Keep Away

JILLIAN LIOTA

Love Is A Verb Books

Book Cover Design and Layout by Blue Moon Creative Studio

Cover Photo © iStock.com/CoffeeAndMilk

ISBN 978-0-9982224-5-5 (paperback)
ISBN 978-0-9982224-3-1 (eBook)
ISBN 978-0-9982224-4-8 (kindle)

to my incredible sister:

you are my inspiration for so many things
you challenge me, you change me, you love me
and when I think of who I want to be when I grow up
I think of you

I love your stupid face forever.

<3

dear reader,
while not all of my works contain difficult subject
matter, I keep a list of content warnings for each of
my books on my website for those who would
like to be prepared for certain topics

for a complete list, please visit:
www.jillianliota.com/content-warnings

CHAPTER ONE
Charlie

September
Five Years Ago

There's a nearly naked man in my room.

A hot one.

Like, really hot.

This is my room, right?

I take a step back and peer at the number on the door I've just opened to make sure I haven't walked into my neighbor's room on accident. Because I've definitely walked into my neighbor Corbin's room by accident and seen him naked.

Oops.

Yup. Red door. #622. Door decorations with our names on them. Charlotte and Rachel, each written on white paper in the shape of a marshmallow, being roasted over a fire. Such a stupid idea. It's never cold enough in Southern California to roast marshmallows. Our RA is such a …

Wait.

My eyes fly back to the nearly-naked man sitting in my room.

He's leaning against my bed, likely because I left mine dropped while my roommate had her bed lofted so she could shove her desk underneath. It takes up way less space, but who really wants to climb up to the top of a bunk bed every day? What are we, ten?

The hot guy is staring at me with a devious little smirk that makes my stomach swoop. But I shake it off, because... well because, yes he may be hot, but he's in my room and he's a stranger.

Ignore the abs, Char.

"I'm concerned that you seem quite comfortable sitting on my bed, in my room, in just your undies, and yet I have no idea who you are," I say, remaining at the door and resting one hand on my hip while the other clutches the knob, readying to slam the door closed and race down the hall to report this person who broke into my room.

But he looks familiar.

And he's gorgeous.

The gorgeous ones always get away with everything. It's actually really obnoxious and maybe I *should* go tell someone that there's a guy in...

"I'm assuming you're the infamous Charlie I've heard so much about," the sex-on-a-stick says, standing from the bed and walking towards me. He puts his hand out as he gets close, towering over me. "I'm Jeremy. Rachel's brother."

I blink.

Then blink again.

Oh.

My.

GOD.

This sexy-ass beast is Rachel's *brother!?* Why didn't she tell me he was so delicious? Well, I guess that would be super gross. If she told me that. So maybe cancel that thought.

I let my eyes shamelessly flick up and down Jeremy's body as I slowly extend my hand to shake his. Bare feet. Muscular calves and thighs with just a touch of a tan line. Blue striped boxer briefs that cling so nicely to his hips. Sexy abs and defined pecs dusted with light brown hair. Not a six pack, but definitely close. Thick arms and toned shoulders. A strong jawline. Brown hair in a faux hawk with buzzed sides. And the most earth shattering blue eyes I've ever seen. Top it all off with a gorgeous smile that's making my knees weak, and we can call this a day, ladies!

Damn, he's gorgeous.

When my eyes finally finish giving him the up-and-down, I notice he's giving me the same once-over, and he doesn't exactly look disappointed. The unrestrained interest he's giving off has me battling a smile.

And we're still shaking hands.

When I realize too much time has passed since either of us has said anything, I gently pull my hand from his and clear my throat.

"I don't know about *infamous*," I say, laughing lightly and passing Jeremy to walk to my dresser on the other side of the room, swaying my hips. "If my sources are correct, you have a much larger reputation around here than little old me."

Once I set my clutch down on my nightstand, slip out of my high heels and turn around, I see Jeremy has returned to his spot leaning against the length of my bed, his long legs stretching out in front of him and crossed at the ankle, his eyes trained on me.

"Sources, huh?" he says with a half smile, drawing my attention to his mouth. "What sources?"

I shrug, feigning ignorance. "A girl's gotta have her secrets," I reply.

But honestly, what am I supposed to say? I know three girls he's hooked up with, and they're all friends with each other, which is kind of gross when you think about it. I know who he is. I've just never matched a face with the name. Which is sad because it is one amazing face.

He's *the* Jeremy Jameson. He's the captain of the soccer team and his name has been tossed around campus frequently enough during my first few weeks at Glendale College that I know without a doubt he's quite the man about campus. But this is the first time I'm seeing him in the flesh. Literally.

I look away from him and take my earrings off, hooking them each carefully into the earring organizer I snagged on clearance from Anthropologie during move-in week.

"And what if I want to know your secrets?" he asks.

I glance at him in the mirror and wonder whether I should be playing hard-to-get. But it's not normally my style, and flirting is much more fun.

"You want to know my secrets?" I ask coyly, running my hands through my hair and pulling the thick locks over one shoulder. When he just nods, I give him a seductive grin. "I don't share secrets with strange men, whether they're in my bed or not."

"So I'm a strange man?" he asks.

"What else would you call a nearly naked man you

4

don't know in your bed?"

"Me? A prank. You? It should be considered an invitation." He bites his lip and re-crosses his arms, drawing my eyes to those muscles.

I give him a sardonic smile. "I typically don't invite men into my bed when I don't know them, but I *do* know a secret or two I can share."

"Oh, really?"

I nod and move towards him, resting my butt on the edge of the bed just a few inches from where he sits. I lean in close, pressing slightly against him. His face is a breath away from mine when I whisper, "RJ snores really loudly."

His head jerks back and he looks at the full smile on my face before barking out a laugh.

"What? Not the secret you were looking for?" I ask.

He shakes his head. "You're crazy if you think that's a secret. We shared a connecting bedroom wall growing up. She's a chainsaw."

I laugh, closing my eyes and thinking about the earplugs I have tucked into my nightstand, the lifesavers that they are.

"Nothing about Rachel is a secret to me," he adds, and I roll my eyes. "What? She's my sister. I know her better than anyone."

"Sorry, mister, but that time has come and gone. You might have known our sweet, little RJ since the day she graced the world with her presence, but *every* girl has secrets. The fact that you call her Rachel when everyone else calls her RJ is just one example of how you might not know her as well as you think."

He rolls his eyes.

"The whole RJ thing is a college thing. She'll always

be Rachel to me."

I laugh. RJ *hates* that he still calls her Rachel.

"And, I can tell you this much," he adds, leaning into me and pushing my hair that has fallen forward back over my shoulder. "Maybe she *can* keep a secret, because she has never mentioned how absolutely *beautiful* you are."

My breath hitches and my stomach swoops.

And my mind takes a moment to just go completely fuzzy like an old TV on the fritz.

Now, let's make something clear. I'm not one of those girls from a teen movie that doesn't realize she's attractive. I know I have a lot going for me. The looks that won me the *Elle Girl* "Make Me a Model" campaign when I was fourteen haven't faded away over the past four years. Rich, silky brunette hair. Big, caramel eyes, and long legs that make shopping for pants a serious hassle, but definitely attract male attention.

At 5'9", I tower over a lot of the women on campus, and a fair share of the men, too. It can make wearing heels feel like overkill, since the 4-inch stilettos I was wearing tonight rock me up to over 6' tall. With the average man sitting at 5'10", I spend most days feeling a bit like a Sasquatch.

But Jeremy? I had to look up when he sauntered over in his bare feet a few minutes ago to shake my hand. That means he's at least 6'3". Six feet and three inches of breathtaking, stunning, startlingly attractive... maleness. And even though I know plenty of guys think I'm *hot*, which was made painfully clear when my fifty-year-old gym teacher commented on it when I was a junior in high school – can we all agree how gross that is? Like, you're married and old enough to be my dad, Mr. Dalton – it's been a long time since someone has called me beautiful.

"But you said I'm *infamous*," I finally get out, leaning away slightly. As much as I'm enjoying being this close to him, it's kind of overwhelming. "What has my sweet roommate told you about me?"

He tilts his head and taps his fingers against his jaw, as if he's trying to recall the memory. "If I remember correctly, you're from Nebraska and you want to be a nurse, right?"

I smile.

"Good memory, but those details hardly make me infamous."

"I may have exaggerated on the infamous part. A little. But I can promise you that moving forward from right now? It's gonna be hard work to forget you."

I let out a small laugh, very much enjoying his ridiculous flattery. "You're just as charming as all the girls say." He blushes slightly. "So tell me, Mr. Jameson, what are *your* secrets?"

He considers me for a second, determining what to share. Maybe trying to figure out my level of trustworthiness. Or trying to decide how to make another innuendo.

"You wanna know a real secret?" I nod. "I've had two professional soccer teams reach out about recruiting me in the past week."

My eyebrows fly up. "Wow, are you serious? I didn't realize Glendale could produce athletes good enough to go pro." The minute the words are out of my mouth, I realize how insulting they are.

"Have you ever been to one of our games?" Jeremy asks, thankfully not seeming upset by my foot-in-mouth moment. When I shake my head he laughs. "Why am I not surprised? If you watched us play, you'd understand. We might be a smaller team, but we're a powerhouse in the college soccer world, regardless of division."

I nod, making a mental note to pay more attention when RJ talks about soccer. And her brother.

"Is RJ excited about it? I mean, she lives and breathes soccer, so I feel like she would be over the moon for you."

He shrugs. "I haven't told her yet, so I'm not really sure."

My brows furrow. "Then why did you tell me?"

He shrugs again, pausing and looking away from me and out the window that showcases the campus quad, before saying, "I don't actually know."

The conversation wilts, then, a silence overtaking the room that is both uncomfortable and yet, at the same time, startlingly calm and soothing.

Growing up attending my parents' dinner parties, I was always told how quickly a lack of conversation could completely tank an evening. I might be from a little town in Nebraska, but I'm also a Davenport. And in the Davenport house, there is no such thing as a comfortable silence. Davenports lead the conversation, or so my mother says. But while she thinks being well-read and knowledgeable about local politics is the best way save the day, I have my own tried-and-true method of furthering along a conversation.

Flirting.

And while flirting with the upper crust of my small town growing up was pretty taxing, trust me when I say that flirting with Jeremy is no hardship.

I clear my throat and lean back towards him. "So, I don't watch a lot of soccer," I say, my voice taking on a slightly different wispy quality. "What position do you play?"

His eyes drop to my mouth, less than a foot from his.

"I'm a striker," he responds, leaning ever-so-slightly towards me.

"What does that mean?"

"It means I power the ball into the net."

"Are you good at it?"

"Oh, Charlie, I'm *so* good at it."

I giggle. "Would you teach me sometime?"

"Oh, I could…"

The door slams open.

"I swear to all that is holy, if you *ever* ask me to do that again… oh, hey Char." RJ's voice and sudden entrance into the room completely shifts the mood.

Her eyes flit quickly between the two of us, huddled next to each other, my body arched towards Jeremy in a seductive curve, his muscles straining as he grips the bed frame, our faces inches from each other.

"Thanks, Rach," Jeremy says, stepping away from our cocoon and over to grab an armful of clothes from RJ. "I owe you one."

RJ huffs, her eyes focused on her brother as he plops his stuff onto her desk and starts sorting through it.

"I don't want to be a part of your hook up protocol, Jer," she says, clearly upset. "Next time, you're out on your ass. Do you know how awkward that was for me? First, to have to go ask Vanessa if I can have my brother's clothes back, and second, to have to ask for it *while her boyfriend is in the room.*"

Jeremy smirks, and I frown a little.

Wait, what?

"I won't ask again, sis. That was a one-time mistake." He shrugs, then grabs his jeans and starts putting them on. "And honestly, it's not my fault. She didn't tell me she had a boyfriend until he barged into the room. Besides, nothing actually happened."

RJ crosses her arms and glares at him. "Did you even ask?"

He stuffs his wallet and phone into his jeans and glances at me. "It seems pointless to ask a girl at a frat party if she's single *after* she makes out with you for thirty minutes."

She waves her hand in the general direction of the hallway. "Well, it's obviously *not* pointless, hence, Vanessa's boyfriend."

"Inappropriate use of the word *hence*, Rach."

She huffs. "No it's not. And don't change the subject. When we get lunch on Monday, we *will* be talking about this."

But I don't think he's paying her any more attention because he's looking back at me. I've barely moved since RJ walked in, but Jeremy's eyes have me shifting slightly where I still stand next to my bed, watching this little sibling spat.

"So, Charlie, I have a question for you." He pulls his shirt over his head, muscles flexing. "You want to be a nurse, right?" I nod. "If I need CPR, can I call you for help?"

I can't help the laughter. It's the most ridiculous pick up line ever, and way overused in the nursing community. But coming from him, it's silly, not nauseating.

Well, at least not to me.

I glance over at RJ mid-laugh and catch her making

gagging faces behind her brother. I guess she doesn't feel the same.

"You know, if the RA catches you here after hours, you'll get in trouble," I say to Jeremy as he slips his feet into his shoes, "and not the type of trouble I can help with."

Jeremy smirks. "Charlie, I think you can help me with any of the troubles I'm currently facing."

I laugh again.

"Alright Jeremy, you've overstayed your welcome." RJ grips Jeremy by the arm and starts dragging him towards the door.

"Fine, fine, I'll take the hint," he says.

"It's not a hint if I'm telling you to get out of my room, you skanky toad."

Jeremy laughs, then wraps his arm around his sister's neck to pull her in for a hug. She melts into him, giving in to the tight embrace, and I feel my own heart squeeze slightly at the sibling affection.

For a brief moment, I let myself think about my sister and brother, and how much I wish the three of us had a relationship like Jeremy and RJ's.

He glances over RJ's head and winks at me, then motions to the door and mouths *five minutes*. "Bye Charlie. Hope to see you again, really soon."

And then he's out the door. Does he want me to follow him? I mean, that's the official *meet me in a second* symbol, right?

But before I can process anything that's happened over the past ten minutes, RJ is right in front of me, looking nervous but determined and oh-so-precious in her glasses and orange and green turtle pajamas.

"Okay, Charlie. Let me make this as clear as possible. I really like you, and I know we've only been living together for a few weeks, but I feel like we could be pretty good friends, so I want to put this out there now." She takes a deep breath. "Jeremy sleeps with... everyone. No repeats, just a good time until it's not."

My mouth drops open and the Davenport in me reaches to clutch the nonexistent pearls around my neck at her boldness.

"I can't tell you what to do, but I think anyone who goes after him is making a mistake. He's a good man and a wonderful brother, but would make a *horrible* boyfriend."

My mouth gapes wider, and I gasp a little. "I mean, I don't even..."

RJ lifts an eyebrow, and being the queen of eyebrow lifting, I know this particular look. It's her *I call bullshit* look.

And then I can't hold it in any longer.

"Okay, first of all, how could you not tell me your brother looks like *that!?*" I say, gesturing to the closed door with both arms in dramatic fashion. "He is the most *gorgeous* man I've ever *seen*! Did you see his abs? And his arms? Oh my god, and his *eyes*. Talk about swoon!"

She makes a gagging face again. "Jer is known around campus for all of those things and then some. I've told you this already. He's like campus royalty or something. It's really annoying." She waves her hand in a way that says it's all hogwash to her.

I clasp my hands together. "*The* Jeremy Jameson. I feel like I need to share this with someone but you're the only person I share things with."

RJ rolls her eyes. "Well, tough. Consider him a topic we just don't talk about. There's politics, religion, and Jeremy."

I laugh as I grab my towel and shower caddie. "But we've talked about politics and religion, weirdo." RJ smiles at me as I slip my feet into flip-flops. "I'm gonna get in a shower while everyone's still at Thirsty Thursdays," I say, walking towards the door.

"You're the weirdo, lusting after my gross brother," she says, then shouts out, "And think about what I said!" as the door closes behind me.

Technically, I head in the direction of the communal showers our floor shares. Quite the adjustment, those communal showers, when you've had a house large enough to never have to share a bathroom. But, also in the direction of the bathroom is the tiny lounge near the stairs. If Jeremy isn't there, I'll shrug it off and take a long hot shower. But if he is...

I peek my head through the lounge door, and a smile creeps onto my face when I see him sitting on one of the red couches, scrolling through his phone.

I clear my throat and lean against the doorway, giving him a flirty smile when his eyes connect with mine.

"You lost, pretty girl?" He says with a wolfish grin, pushing up off the couch and walking towards me, tucking his phone into his front pocket.

I shrug.

"Need me to help you with anything?"

I shrug again, trying to restrain my smile and failing miserably.

And then he's standing in front of me, so close. Toe to toe, breath to breath.

Jeremy lifts his hand and lightly touches my arm, tracing a pattern down until he reaches my hand, then flirts his fingers with mine. Normally, guys giving me attention provides a little ego boost and nothing more. But this light-touching thing has my pulse racing and my temperature increasing rapidly. I can feel the blood rushing to my chest and neck, surely causing my skin to flush red. Traitorous Irish heritage.

"Look at that blush," he says in a low tone, barely more than a whisper. "Tell me, pretty girl, how far down does that blush spread?"

I'm certain that my skin has turned beat red, but I'm also shockingly woozy and my breathing turns hard as he leans forward slowly, until his face hovers just at the space where my neck meets my shoulder. My eyes drop closed and I just try to memorize the feel of him so close to me like this.

"Let me take you out, Charlotte. I bet we'll have a really good time," he says, his breath scattering goose bumps along my collarbone.

I barely manage to nod and utter an *uh huh* before he's taking a step back. When I open my eyes, he's standing there, looking slightly off-kilter, and I think I see something deeper than lust in his eyes. But then he's back to the smirking, and he hands his phone over for me to enter my number. After I've punched it in, he fiddles around with it.

"I just called you. So now you'll know who it is when I text you."

I smile. "So when is this happening?"

"Tomorrow."

"Really? You're not gonna ask if I have plans?"

He reaches for my hand and lays a light kiss on the inside of my wrist, which feels at odds with the way he's staring at me, his gaze smoldering. "Do I sound like a dick if I say you'll cancel them if you have plans tomorrow?"

His eyes twinkle.

Should I find that arrogant and egotistical? Yes. Do I? *Eye roll.* I can't be pissed just because he knows I'm interested. I know how to flirt with the best of them, but like I said, hard-to-get isn't my thing.

I shake my head slightly. "A dick, maybe, but not a liar."

He smiles.

"See you tomorrow, Char."

He winks once, then walks out of the lounge. I hear the stairwell door open, his heavy feet echoing on the concrete steps, before it closes behind him.

I wander in a haze to the bathroom on our floor, and barely remember the shower I take. It's going to be a long night of no sleep for me.

CHAPTER TWO
Charlie

September
Five Years Ago

Jeremy: *Meet me by the stairs out front. I'll be there in 5.*

I grin to myself.

I shouldn't be this elated about going out on a date with a guy who I know hooks up casually with any girl that flirts his way. But I can't help it. The excitement that races through me at the sound of a simple text from him is more than I've felt in terms of excitement for a date since Hamilton Sowell asked me to the prom.

And I can't for the life of me figure out why I'm so damn giddy. He's clearly the most attractive guy that's ever asked me out, by like, a mile. But I don't know if it's just how hot he is. I mean, I get asked out a lot, and I usually say yes, as long as the guy peaks my interest with his looks or his humor.

As horrible as it sounds, sometimes I say yes just

because I like chatting with new people. When you meet new people, there is usually some genuine interest in getting to know each other. And I love that look some guys get when they seem to eat up every word I have to say.

I sigh as I watch myself in the mirror.

Even thinking things like that makes me feel like a self-centered asshole. I guess when you grow up never getting to be yourself, even the smallest amount of attention is like throwing a match onto gasoline.

But this date with Jeremy feels... different than the others I've had since I started dating. And I can't figure out why.

I finish adding my lipstick in the mirror on my dresser, where I've been standing for the past hour working on my hair and makeup. I love this stuff. I love the way it looks and the way it makes me feel. After spending my junior high and high school years under the watchful eye of my mother, who had very particular tastes about appropriate makeup – muted colors, light mascara and definitely no eyeliner – the freedom of being away at college has been such a breath of fresh air. I love being able to do it up the way I want.

And this maroon lipstick I got on sale at MAC is fucking *boss*.

I finish slicking it on, dab a bit onto tissue paper, then smile to make sure nothing's on my teeth. I move over to the full-length mirror that hangs on the back of the door and give myself a once-over. I've always been one of the girls that can put in just the right amount of effort to look good without looking like I'm trying too hard. Today, I didn't find that balance and I am totally okay with it.

I have outdone myself.

My hair falls in curls and waves down to the middle of my back in that "oh, I've just come back from a day at the beach, but I have a personal stylist who takes care of my hair, so no worries" look that graces so many magazine covers.

My makeup is flawless.

My skinny jeans have the right amount of rip mid-thigh on my right and at the knee on my left, and while they might be too short because I bought them at a thrift shop, my choice to cuff them above the ankle and pair them with a pair of dark green ankle boots makes it look intentional. A black and white striped shirt and a green jacket, and I know I've got a great first date look.

I quickly remind myself that I shouldn't expect this to be the first of many. That's probably unlikely.

But a girl can dream.

I put in some faux-pearl earrings, spritz myself with some body spray and grab my bag, then head down to the lobby to wait for Jeremy.

I'm walking out of the building when he pulls up. I take a few steps down as Jeremy climbs out of his midnight blue Ford Bronco. It's an old-school ride, and I *love* how he looks climbing out of it. Tan jeans, purple button up, black keds, silver watch, hair neat and tidy but slightly askew in that look guys have when they look like they've been running their hands through it.

And a gorgeous smile aimed right at me.

"Hey there, pretty girl," he says as he gives me a perusal. "I have to say, you look absolutely breathtaking."

My chest tightens at his use of the word. I'm used to being the hot girl. It might make me sound like a bitch, but I can't help genetics. But, breathtaking? That is not a word men use with me. Or at least, not a word the boys I've spent time with have used. I'm sure I blush from head to toe.

He walks towards me and takes my hand with a smile, then leads me around to the passenger side and opens the door.

I touch his shirt collar before I step into the bronc. "You clean up pretty nicely yourself, sir."

He bites his lip and I force myself to turn away and climb in, setting my bag at my feet.

Once we're on the road, I turn in my seat to look at Jeremy. "So, where are we headed? All you said was dressy casual."

He smirks and flicks the blinker, merging us into the lane that leads to the freeway. "Wouldn't *you* like to know?"

"Well… yes, that's why I asked."

He looks to me and I laugh, then he follows. "Well, it's a secret. So you'll just have to accept that, okay?"

I nod, then turn my head to watch the road. He drives the car onto the freeway and I see the large green sign that says we're headed towards downtown Los Angeles. Being without a car, it's quite a treat to get out of Glendale. I love the area, and in just the few weeks I've been here, I've found Glendale to be incredibly charming, with lots of little boutique shops. And the Glendale Galleria is so amazing that I've been there four times already. Always to browse, never to buy. But it's almost just as fun.

"So, what made you want to be a nurse?" Jeremy asks, clicking buttons on the radio until he's satisfied with the music that sits on low.

I smile something wistful and think about the reasons,

trying to sort it out in a way that's brief but comprehensive. "I have an amazing grandmother. My Nan was a huge influence in my life, and when she got on in years, my parents put her in a home because they didn't want to deal with her. I was so mad when they chose to not only put her in a home, but also send her away from Nebraska. We visited Nan one time when I was sixteen, and I was so angry when I saw how little the nursing staff cared about their patients."

I turn in my seat, leaning my shoulder and head against the back, looking at Jeremy. "Can you imagine? Getting to an age where you can't really take care of yourself anymore, and you get shipped off to somewhere far from everything you know, where you don't know anyone, and the people treat you like shit?" I shake my head. "I promised myself I would be someone who made sure as many people as possible got to live out their last years in a positive environment."

"Your Nan, she still in that place that treated her bad?" he asks, one eyebrow up, eyes still on the road.

"No, thank god," I say on an exhale. "I pitched a huge fit and my parents agreed to move her. They've got plenty of money, and I told them it was the least they could do to make sure she was in a good place. So they moved her to the Pasadena Village, which is much swankier. They have beauty pageants and yearbooks and take them on trips to museums and stuff."

Jeremy smiles. "Lemme guess... does that have something to do with you picking Glendale for college?"

I smile back, then tap my nose and point a finger at him. "Look at *you* with your illustrious powers of deduction. Color me impressed, sir."

He laughs. "Ass."

I shrug. "Yeah, pretty much."

Jeremy clicks his blinker again and shifts over to the right so we can hop onto a new freeway.

"The driving in California kills me," I say, resting my head on the headrest. "I don't know how you do it." When he laughs I slap his arm playfully. "Don't laugh, it's ridiculous. I mean… look, this freeway has *ten lanes* all the way across. That is *insane.*"

He laughs again. "Well, when you grow up with it, you don't know any different. I visited a friend of mine in Indiana once and the road from his town into Indianapolis was two lanes, one on each side. He said I drive like an asshole, and I said everyone there drives like their car tops out at fifty."

"Nebraska's the same, although you definitely get the people on the roads in more rural parts who think it's cool to drag race down both sides of the highway. Now *that's* asshole."

"You miss it?" he asks, and I can tell he really means it, so I need to really mean what I say back.

I pause, mulling it over, really thinking about the family I left behind. The house that felt like a stuffy museum, the rules that made me want to crawl out of my skin, the constant battle of not wanting to disappoint my family while still wanting to be true to myself.

"Sometimes I do," I finally respond. Then he looks over at me and I'm hit with the full force of Jeremy Jameson, his face just slightly concerned but open, his hand resting casually on the wheel at the wrist like men do when they feel comfortable.

"But not today," I add. "Today, I don't miss it at all."

I love the smell of the ocean. I've only seen it one time, and that was back when we visited Nan when I was sixteen. I'd had to beg my parents to take us, and they'd acted so put-out about it, like seeing the ocean was some small thing that could happen any day of the week.

Not when you live in fucking *Nebraska*, mom and dad.

They took us to Venice Beach because it was close to the airport, and we got a total of fifteen minutes out on the sand, just staring at the water, before they grabbed my siblings and I, shoved us back into our chauffeured car and directed the driver to take us to LAX.

It should have been the first thing I did when I got here for college, but with the full-on week of orientation events, followed immediately by the first week of classes and the fact I'm carless, I've unfortunately only been able to see the ocean from the plane when I landed at LAX back in August.

So when Jeremy pulls off the freeway at a sign that indicates we're headed towards Venice beach, I nearly shoot out of my seat with excitement. And the smile on his face, that wavers somewhere between smug and honestly pleased, only grows the closer we get.

"Now, I know Venice Beach is kind of touristy. But Rachel mentioned at lunch last week that you'd been wanting to go to the beach," he says as he parallel parks on a residential street a few blocks from the water.

My face is nearly breaking off of my body with how huge my smile is, and I hop out of the Bronco as Jeremy just laughs and puts the car in park. I inhale deeply, loving that beach smell and soaking it in, memories rushing back of me with my sister and brother standing side-by-side, just staring at the ocean.

My sister, Isobel, two years older than me, holding my hand. My sweet brother, Grey, a year younger than me, trying to act cool but vibrating with as much excitement as his growing body was willing to allow, tucked in under my arm and holding on tight. We'd been close as long as I could remember, me and Grey. Irish twins is the term, when you're less than a year apart from a sibling. Issy and I were as close as she was willing to allow, considering the distance she always seemed to place in between herself and the rest of the family.

But that day at the beach? That fifteen minutes when we stood together and stared in awe at the mass of blue that made the air feel sticky and sweet at the same time? That was a perfect memory that I keep close to my heart.

And now, getting to experience it with Jeremy, I feel like a little kid. For once in my life, my thoughts of being impressive and sexy and alluring are nowhere in the recesses of my mind. I don't care what he thinks as I grab his hand and race to get to the water. I don't care what *anyone* thinks as I barrel rudely through the masses of people that are filling the boardwalk, Jeremy's hand in mind, his laughter spilling out of him in deep thunders that only build my excitement.

And then, suddenly, I'm in the sand. Practically in the same place I looked at the ocean with my siblings. Jeremy is at my side, still chuckling lightly and adjusting his hand in mine – not taking it away, just threading our fingers together and giving it a squeeze.

"I'm excited," I whisper, trying to catch my breath.

"You don't say," he responds, the sparkle in his eyes when I look to him reflecting that whatever he just witnessed from me is something he enjoyed.

"I've never touched the ocean before," I say, my eyes returning to the water in the distance that's no longer so distant.

"I'm actually kind of scared."

"Don't worry, sweet stuff," he replies, bumping his hip with mine and lifting our joined hands to his mouth, kissing mine lightly. "I'll stay with you the whole time."

I nod without looking at him, knowing his eyes are on me. I bend over and slip out of my boots, and then I start walking at a normal pace out to the water, my feet sinking into the sand that's starting to cool as the sun begins to set, Jeremy's hand still linked with mine.

When we are about ten feet away from where the waves rush onto the shore, I stop.

"It's so big," I whisper, in absolute awe at how there's just ocean and ocean as far as my eyes can see.

"I feel like this is an important moment, so I shouldn't say it, but I'm going to. *That's what she said.*"

My head whips to look at Jeremy, who has a sheepish smile on his face, and I burst into laughter. Jeremy joins me, and we spend at least a minute letting our giggles subside.

"Thanks for that. Ass," I finally say, when I can get the words out.

He shrugs. "I mean, *that's what she said* jokes are perfect for every occasion."

"Sure they are."

"No seriously," he replies. "Your friend's grandmother is in the hospital, the nurse can't find the vein and the grandmother screams for them to just stick it in already? *That's what she said.*"

I laugh again, still holding Jeremy's hand in one but clutching my stomach with the other, dropping my shoes in the sand.

"You're standing next to your wife at her friend's funeral and she whispers that it's just so hard? *That's what she said.*"

"How old are you?" I ask mid-laugh.

Then I let out a shriek as cold water rushes over my toes, and I grip Jeremy's hand even tighter. "What the fuck!" I shout through another giggle. "Why is it so cold?" I look behind me and then back at the water. "And how did we get so close to the water?"

Jeremy is smiling softly as I squeeze the life out of his hand. "You seemed scared, so I thought if I could distract you while I moved us closer to the water, it wouldn't be so bad."

"Well aren't you just the cutest?" I say, leaning into him, my thoughts no longer on the big ocean in front of us and instead on the thoughtful man next to me.

He extracts his fingers from mine and wraps his arm around my shoulders, tugging me close and resting his cheek on the top of my head.

"I am pretty cute," he says, eliciting another laugh from me, this one more subdued.

We stand there for a few minutes, just taking in the sights and smells and sounds. I should be focused on the fact that I finally touched the ocean for the first time in my life, the cool water washing against me, the feel of the sand between my toes and the handful of birds in the air, or the sounds of the boardwalk in the distance.

But all I can process is the feel of his strong arm wrapped around me, and the smell of his cologne, clean and slightly woody. I turn from the water and wrap my arms around his stomach, pressing my cheek to his chest, inhaling the salt and sea and the smell of him. Jeremy's arms tighten around me for a moment before he tilts my head up so we are looking at each other, his eyes searching mine.

And then he dips down and presses his lips against mine, his kiss at odds with the gentle and caring way he'd been holding me in his arms. But that thought passes quickly as our mouths open against each other, tongues searching and licking, the kiss deep and wet, pulling the breath from my lungs. His hands are in my hair, holding me close to him, and then one drops and presses on my ass, pushing our bodies even closer together until we are molded together. He moans into my mouth and then pulls from me, panting slightly and resting his forehead against mine.

His eyes are searching my face, his expression cloudy, so unlike the jokester from just moments before. I don't know what to say apart from something stupid like *are you going to keep kissing me now?* or *can you put your hands back on my butt?* So I hug him tightly and put my cheek back to his chest, listening to the steady but rapid thump of his heart.

"Where's your phone?" he asks.

I scrunch my brows at the random question. "In my purse in the car I think."

And then all I see is sand and Jeremy's legs, because he's lifted me up and thrown me over his shoulder, and is running into the water.

"What are you doing!?" I shriek, as I feel spray from where Jeremy's legs are smacking through the water shooting up onto me.

"Time to cool off, sweet stuff," he says just before he slides me forward and we both go under.

CHAPTER THREE
Charlie

September
Five Years Ago

"Okay, so in hindsight, maybe throwing us into the water fully clothed wasn't the best idea," Jeremy says with an apologetic smile.

"You think?" I say, sitting on the tailgate of his Bronco, towel-drying my hair with a shirt that was in one of the several gym bags Jeremy has in his car.

I'm trying to act cool. I'm trying to be calm. So... I'm drenched in ocean water on the date I've been the most excited about in forever. The Davenport inside of me won't allow me to make him feel uncomfortable for throwing me into the water. I mean, he doesn't understand the time and attention that went into the hair and makeup and outfit selection for this date. It's not like he did it on purpose, and he probably wouldn't have done it if he knew it would bother me.

I take a breath. In. Then out.

But on the inside, I am so not cool. I feel completely

thrown off my game, and incredibly conscious of the fact that I now have raccoon eyes and smell like a wet dog. I mean, *come on!* I wanted so badly for this date to be perfect and now I feel gross. How am I supposed to make a great impression when I look like a swamp creature!?

So I take another breath. *Lighten the mood, Char.*

"If I smelled that bad, you could have just taken me to a pharmacy to grab some deodorant or something." I add a smile to set him at ease.

He chuckles, his muscles flexing under a workout shirt he pulled on after we got back to the car. "If I'd thought far enough ahead, maybe I would have told you to wear a little bikini." His eyebrows go up and down. "Now that, pretty girl... that's something I wouldn't mind seeing any day of the week."

His eyes linger on my face and I'm suddenly in equal parts hyper-aware of how I look and wanting to hide, as well as dying for him to move closer to me and kiss me again *regardless* of how I look.

I shrug, slowly allowing myself a chance to get back into a flirty mood, where I'm far more comfortable. "Well, if you had just asked, I could have stripped down to my panties before you heaved me into the ocean."

He gives me a roguish grin. "You are such a tease."

I just shrug and give him a playful look. "Am I teasing?"

He chuckles, then steps into my space, his arms braced on the bed of the truck, his face inches from mine.

"Wanna know why I threw us into the water?" he asks, pressing a small kiss to the side of my neck. Before I can respond, he answers his own question. "Because if I hadn't, I might have gotten us arrested for public indecency."

I let out a shaky sigh as he shifts and kisses the other side of my neck.

"Well it's good you beat me to it. I'm basically a WWE fighter, and I don't know if your ego could have handled me body slamming you into the water."

His lips freeze, planted on my collarbone, and then his forehead falls forward onto my shoulder and he starts shaking with silent laughter.

I smile, enjoying that I've made him laugh. But I still feel entirely off my game with him. Normally, I go full-on flirt. I don't know where this goof-ball joke teller came from or why she's hijacking my date. But I can't seem to stop being *silly* with him. And if I'm honest, I really like it.

His head finally lifts and the smile there is soft and genuine.

"Like I said. A tease."

"Well, someone needs to be the comedic relief, so please consider me your jester for the evening."

"Really?" I nod. "Okay, gimme some one-liners, then."

I shake my head. "Sorry, Charlie. They come out when the mood strikes. You'll just have to wait and see."

"Charlie is *your* name."

"Yeah, I know. But it's not *my* fault the saying sounds weird when coming from someone named Charlie. Like, if someone named Deborah called you a Debbie Downer. Or if someone named Nellie called you a Nervous Nellie." I put my hands in the air in a *what can you do* gesture.

He rolls his eyes playfully, then grabs my jeans off the door of the truck bed and starts wringing the water out of them.

"Thanks for the backup clothes, by the way," I add, resting my elbows on my criss-crossed legs and my face in my hands, watching him. "I definitely think these gray sweat pants and green shirt that says," I pull it forward and slowly read it upside down with a giggle, "*World's Okayest Runner,* are much sexier and will be much more likely to turn you on than the outfit I was wearing before. Especially since I'll still be wearing my dope-ass *boots!*" I finish with a flourish by kicking out my legs to show them off. "I mean, they match the shirt, so..."

Jeremy's face has a smile on it as he pulls his wet wallet from his jeans pocket and sets it in the enclosed bed of the Bronco, next to his ruined watch. But it doesn't look completely genuine. He looks... if I'm totally honest? A little constipated.

And just like that, any frustration I felt at him for throwing us into the deep blue drains from my body. I might look disgusting, but I can't let him feel bad about being spontaneous. I mean, isn't that something I usually admire in people?

"Hey," I say, waiting for his eyes to meet mine. And when they do, I know that I couldn't be upset at him anymore even if I wanted to. "I'm not mad about the dip in the water. I promise." I reach over and rest my hand on his. "I'd rather be dripping wet with you than dry with someone else."

The minute the words come out of my mouth, his eyes widen and he looks like he's choking on a laugh.

I roll my eyes, but can't help the giggle that pops from my mouth. "Okay," I say, drawing out the word, wishing I could be flirty and dirty in this moment but struggling to find something to say. "So what's next, mister?" I decide that moving this date along is the best course of action. Would I prefer an hour or two to get myself back to what I deem date-worthy in hair and make up? Yes. Do I have that? No. So my choice is to suck it up and enjoy the evening, or pout like a little asshole and make him take us home.

I hop off the tailgate and strike a pose, "We strutting our fine selves down the boardwalk?"

He pauses to look at me. "You're still up to wander around?"

I furrow my brow. "Did you not see the complete insanity that was my reaction to coming here? I may be in sweats and boots, smell like a dog, and have mascara dripping down my face, but I will *not* give up on this extravaganza." I throw my hands into the air. "I am here to be entertained!"

He smiles and nods, chucking the rest of our stuff into the back of the Bronco. "Well, then. We can't disappoint the lady."

I huff. "Of course we can't."

"My god, does it ever stop?" he says with a laugh, closing up and locking the doors.

I just point to myself. "I told you. Jester."

He grabs my hand and we start walking to the boardwalk, chatting about all things random. The more we walk and talk, the more I see Jeremy's flirty confidence return. He eyes me up and down, flirts his fingers with mine, rests his hands on my hips… I'm getting smacked with a wall of in-your-face interest. And in reality? I don't entirely know how to respond.

In the past, I was the one with the confidence, the

one doing the flirty thing with the guys. I'd touch their shoulder or smooth out their hair, or brush past them just slightly. It was an ego boost, for sure. And the guys ate it up.

But Jeremy... he's this entirely different breed of man that my eighteen-year-old self hasn't come across before. He reeks of confidence, but every so often there is the hint of vulnerability there too. I can tell he's a man who likes to be in control, which feeds the kid inside of me who lived in an overly controlled environment, and he looks just a bit frazzled when he *isn't* in control of the situation. I know how horrible that feels, too.

So, now that I'm faced with the reality of his confidence and flirtation, I feel a bit more nervous. Heaps more overwhelmed than I had originally felt when agreeing to this date.

Ugh, get out of your head, Charlotte. Just enjoy this date with the hottest guy you've ever had acknowledge your presence.

The cool thing about visiting a place like Venice Beach is that it's filled with weirdos, so no one looks twice at you if you're in sweats and sexy boots. I find that the more he talks to me – like now, about how he got into playing soccer – the less concerned I am about what other people think I look like.

After a while of wandering outside, I spot an independent bookstore and lead us inside. When I see the Clearance section, I make a beeline straight for it. I'm not a big reader, but I love do-it-yourself books. Not things like "Weight Loss for Dummies" or "Anybody Can Be Cool... But Awesome Takes Practice" – which is a real book I found once, no joke. I'm more about the ones that teach you to crochet or make loom potholders with the illustrative photos and bright colors. It's how I got really into hair and makeup. There was this tiny bookstore in my hometown of Kilburn that had Bookworm Wednesdays, and all of the clearance books would drop to a dollar or less.

We had tons of money growing up. If I'd asked my mom for any new toy or gadget or, when I got into my teen years, a new car or a trip into Omaha to go shopping at the outlets, there wouldn't have been an issue. But ask her for money to buy do-it-yourself books? I'd tried that once.

"Why would you pay for books to learn how to do it when you can just pay a person to do it instead?"

Yeah, that conversation had been scintillating.

So any time my mom would give me money for something, and she said to keep the change, I'd take the coins and toss them into an empty shoebox in my closet. And on Wednesdays after school, I'd head to The Bookworm Shoppe and browse. I rarely ever bought anything, but I did find some great books on doing smoky eyes and really interesting braids. Sure, I could have just watched YouTube tutorials, but there was something satisfying about tucking my new-to-me book into my backpack and then returning home, knowing I was going to wait for mom and dad to go to some dinner or swanky thing to crack it open and practice.

Grey always sat and watched me, helping some of the time, even knowing his friends would have teased him mercilessly about doing hair and makeup with his sister. But Issy would huff and storm off, frustrated that I was breaking the rules – again – and probably going to get away with it – again.

There's always a thrill I get when digging through clearance bins at bookstores. Even finding older books that have women with hair like Farrah Fawcett's, I still can't help but smile.

I'm running my fingers along the clearance shelves for who knows how long when I bump into someone.

"Sorry." I look up and finding Jeremy's eyes on me. "Oh my god." I clutch my hands together and press them to my mouth. "How long was I zoned out?" I ask, speaking through my fingers, my eyes wide.

He smiles. "Only about fifteen minutes. No big deal. I had fun watching you. You were *very* focused."

I laugh through my hands and exhale a breath, glad that he isn't offended. "I get *really* into this sometimes," I say. "I love hair and makeup, and some of these old-school supermodels have classic looks that never go out of style.

He steps towards me. It's just a normal step, nothing rushed or calculated about it, but I can't help the hitch to my breath at his sudden nearness. Maybe it's because we're in a slightly darker corner, or because I'm suddenly pressed up against the bookshelf behind me. Regardless, the surge of energy that flows through my body when he gets close to me… it's a heady feeling.

He leans down, bracing an arm on the bookshelf, right by my face. "I've never understood why so many women have to cake their faces to feel beautiful," he says, his eyes searching, flitting over my nose, my cheeks, my lips. " You wanna talk about classic beauty?" he asks. His other hand tilts my chin up. "I bet the most beautiful thing in the world would be your face, completely naked, waking up in the morning."

I'm caught up entirely in his reference to me being naked – even if it is just about my face, because, let us all be completely honest here, he's *not* just talking about my face. I'm so caught up in what he said, that I don't realize he's waiting for me to respond, his face inches from mine.

"Well…" I finally choke out, feeling a whole lot flustered. "Well… yup."

Yup? Get it together!

"I mean… yes, that does sound…" I clear my throat, but I just can't seem to say anything.

He chuckles, then leans down and presses a soft kiss against my neck, which is rapidly becoming my new favorite thing. I close my eyes, breath in, and try to calm my racing heart.

"Having trouble coming up with a response, are we?" he asks, and when I open my eyes, I see the twinkle in his.

I let out a breath, then lift up slightly, our noses touching, our breaths mingling.

"Sorry about that," I say, bringing my hands up to press them against his chest. I slowly run them up and down his torso, and delight in the feeling I get when his eyes flare at my boldness. "I got a little caught up in the visual of what would happen *before* waking up in your bed."

He stares at my lips. "I never said my bed."

I shrug a shoulder, watching my hand stroke his shirt. "Oops. I forgot. I meant to say a towel on the beach. That *is* what you meant earlier when you said public indecency, right?"

He smiles, a slightly devilish little thing, then lets out a little laugh, shaking his head. "What am I gonna do with you?"

I move my mouth to his ear and whisper, "I thought that's what we were just talking about."

Then I side-step and duck under his arm, which is still planted on the bookshelf, and begin walking over to the register.

CHAPTER FOUR
Jeremy

September
Five Years Ago

I watch her walk away from me, her hips swaying, and I realize I have gotten myself into quite the predicament.

This girl is hot – like, flaming hot Cheetos dusted with ghost peppers hot – no question. Being my sister's roommate added a bit of the forbidden factor. Not gonna lie, that shit can be quite the turn on. And if I'm reading her correctly, she's pretty down for whatever happens tonight.

Normally, these pieces would be enough for me to start moving things along. My typical M.O. with women is pretty consistent. Flirt and be charming in whatever way that works for them.

I'm not trying to be manipulative, and the girls I go out with know the score. They know it's just a fling, nothing serious. So they get it when I lay on the charm, because they know what they're in for when I take them out, which is typically the same thing they're looking for.

I'm not saying *every* date ends in the bedroom (or car, or limo, or club bathroom stall), but I do have a pretty high success rate, and trust me when I say the ladies never leave wanting.

So I flirt and charm. We grab a meal or a drink or go dancing. And then things move back to my place or hers, a hotel or a private spot. She gets off, I get off, and then we're done. I mean, that's pretty standard procedure for most guys I know. So I've never seen anything wrong with it before.

And here's where my predicament comes in.

I'm not entirely sure where this date is going.

Shit, don't get me wrong – I'm having a blast. On top of the stuff I mentioned before, Charlotte Davenport is also a really nice person, and she makes me laugh. I've never been a particularly laughy guy, and I've laughed like, at least ten times since I picked her up a few hours ago. Not only that, but there's this feeling I've been having where I feel like I could tell her… anything.

So, a part of me wants to wrap this up and take her back to my place – because we both know her room at Glendale College isn't an option. Why put it off when she keeps hinting that she's down?

I have no fucking clue.

Maybe I know this isn't gonna go anywhere, but I love her company, so I'm delaying moving things along?

Maybe I wonder if someone as sweet as her, regardless of her expert flirting, is someone I *should* take home at all?

Or… maybe I'm considering just taking her home and scheduling another date?

And that's when I get those film zoom scenes. You know, when the camera zooms in on the character and the background zooms out, super fast, in a moment of shock or realization.

And my moment of realization?

I'm not sure I'm in this for a romp in the hay.

Sure, that may have been where things initiated. Any man that looks at Charlie and doesn't think about sex is absolutely insane, and I know things between us would be so hot.

But I can't really process this other feeling I'm having. This feeling that rushing things along would be a mistake. That spending time with her might be more than a casual fling. That it could be something special and meaningful.

And that's why I'm in a predicament. I literally have no idea what I'm doing.

Sure, my confidence and charm come out full force. It's natural. But earlier, when we were talking about what made me get into soccer? I felt like I could really *talk* to her. Tell her the nerves I've been feeling with the recruiting season coming up for MLS teams. Or my fears about leaving Rachel behind when I move away to play professionally.

Because it will happen. I hope. I try to be as confident as possible, mainly because big egos are what makes professional sports fun to watch. You don't become a Beckham or a Messi or a Ronaldo without some serious fucking certainty that you rock on the field.

I sigh and watch her pay for her book at the register, finally following behind her after standing like an idiot in the clearance section and just watching her from a distance.

She turns once she's finished and flashes me that absolutely gorgeous smile of hers. I know she feels self-conscious about how she looks right now, but I think she's way more beautiful without all of that stuff on her face. It makes her seem softer somehow.

I may have no idea what I'm doing, but she doesn't seem to be too upset about it. So I smile back at her, take her hand in mine, and lead us out of the store.

"So, tell me about what it was like growing up with RJ," she says, as we wander aimlessly through the throngs of people that populate the Venice Boardwalk every day. "I mean, I'm really enjoying living with her, but she seems like kind of a closed book."

I nod. "Yeah, she's always been like that. I love that girl so much, but it's hard to open up to people when you've spent your entire life living in the embarrassing shadow of our dad."

She looks to me with a crease in her brow. "What's the deal with him? RJ hasn't mentioned him at all. When we were getting to know each other she would only refer to you as her family."

I give a pained smile at that.

"Yeah, he's pretty much a raging alcoholic. The kind of dad that scares other families. It's hard to be a kid and want to play with your friends, and then find out they're not allowed to come to your house. RJ had a handful of friends when she was younger, but she pushed a bunch of them away. I've never really understood why, but everyone responds differently to pain, I guess."

Charlie gives me a sweet smile. "I'm sure having you around helped. I've heard her extol the virtues of her amazing brother.

I let out a laugh at that. "I don't know about amazing. I mean, I try to be a good brother but I'm never sure if

I'm getting it right. In some ways, I act a bit more like her dad than her brother, which she doesn't appreciate."

Charlie giggles. "I'm sure she loves having you around."

"I hope so. I get lunch with her almost every week, I even used to do it when she was still in high school, but it was a monthly thing. It petered out her senior year because she got so busy, but we picked it back up as soon as she moved in mid-summer to do that early arrivals course."

I pause as we take a seat on a bench.

"So, while we enjoy spending time together, we are both basically waiting to see what happens next."

"What will that be like when you get... what is it? Drafted?"

"The SuperDraft, yeah," I supply, referring to the name of the period of time in January when the MLS teams will start picking their players. I rub my hand against the back of my neck. I guess that thing about wanting to share with her how I feel is coming to the fore-front. Part of me wants to brush it off, but...

"I mean, I'll get drafted, no doubt," I say, pushing forward that confidence. "The good thing is that I'll have a full-time job, with a full-time salary. So I can visit her and she can visit me, no problems."

Charlie nods. "Well, that's good. But I mean, it'll be the first time you live more than a few hours from each other, right? Like, it's not like you can just hop in a car and go see her for a day if you live in Maine."

"Okay, first of all, there are no teams in Maine. And I don't know if I could live somewhere that cold," I say with a laugh. "But you're right, it would be very different."

Taking a breath, I decide to launch into it. "The reality is that the chances are around five percent that I'll end up in LA."

"That's… pretty specific."

"Yeah, my coach and I have run the numbers on this, a few times. There's twenty-three teams in the league, and the order of pick is based on who was the worst the year before. Coach is pretty certain that I'll go in the end of the first round or the beginning of the second, which would mean I would be tapped by either a top ranked team or a shitty team. The teams in LA are one of each."

I run my hands through my hair in mild frustration. "The problem, though, is that teams also pick based on positions they need filled. And both LA teams have a pretty full load when it comes to the position I play. So, the higher ups will probably find it more important to go after players in positions they need to fill first to make sure they get higher quality."

"Wow," she says. "I never watch sports, but I'm really impressed that you'd do all the research on all of that. Like, that's amazing. Doesn't that help with some of the nerves?"

I shake my head. "Not at all," I laugh out. When she joins me I feel a bit of the tension drain from my shoulders. "Last year, one of the best teams traded away a pick and ended up picking someone who had already been in conversations with another team. It caused quite an storm."

"So even though your chances are technically five percent, it could be higher just because someone decides to do something weird?" she asks.

I laugh again. "Yeah, something like that."

"Seems shitty to have to leave your future up to someone else," she says. It seems like an off-handed remark, but the way her eyes look out at the beach, slightly lost and searching, when she'd been previously so focused on me… it's about more than me.

"Hey," I say, and she turns to look back at me. "I know what I'm getting myself into, and it's just par for the course. Every player goes through this. The worry and fear about what's next. Wondering when they'll get drafted." I shrug. "I mean really, no matter how much I plan and prepare, and I've done a lot of it, we are all slaves to the big machine, right? Isn't this how nursing is going to be, too? At some point you'll have to apply for jobs and hope you get the one you want. But maybe you won't and you'll have to get excited about a different opportunity."

"Oh lord, please don't remind me," she says, that smile returning to her face.

I smile back at her. "My point is, things happen in life, good and bad, easy and hard. To all of us. And what's important is learning how to adapt to it."

I love the nod she gives me, like she really gets what I'm talking about.

Hell, I'm surprised I make sense right now.

I've never really shared any of this with anyone before, but that beautiful smile of hers is so disarming. I feel like I could tell her anything.

"So, long story longer, I'm nervous about moving away from RJ. I just know it's gonna happen, and I don't know how either of us are gonna cope."

"Well, you seem to have a great relationship, so I'm sure no matter what happens, you'll both figure it out."

I smile at her positivity. It's really refreshing.

"Well, I think it's time for dinner, don't you? I made a reservation."

Her face falls, and a part of me wants to laugh, because I know she's concerned about how she looks.

"Don't worry about it," I add. "We'll be totally fine."

I grab her hand and start walking us down the boardwalk. Time for a sunset view.

CHAPTER FIVE
Charlie

September
Five Years Ago

"Are you sure we're allowed to be here?" I ask, taking a seat on the surprisingly comfortable patio couch.

"Don't worry," Jeremy replies, taking a seat next to me and wrapping his arm around my shoulders. "It's going to be okay."

"But we look like shit," I say back, causing Jeremy to bark out a laugh.

"Pretty girl, I doubt you've ever looked like shit in your entire life."

I blush slightly and tuck my legs up onto the couch, leaning into Jeremy's chest to hide my face.

"Oooooh, are we suddenly shy?" he says, playfully, tugging me back to look at me.

I can't help the smile that takes over my face. "Hush," I respond, then curl back into him.

When Jeremy told me we were still going to take advantage of our dinner reservation, I'm pretty sure the look on my face said it all. It wouldn't matter where the reservation was. Our post-plunge outfits weren't exactly restaurant material. I can say with everything I am that a Davenport has never gone out to dinner looking like I do right now.

But he insisted, so I went along with it, certain we would be turned away. But apparently Jeremy is friends with the manager of this rooftop bar in Venice Beach. After Greg got a good laugh at our clothes, he took us up to the top.

Where my breath was immediately stolen from my lungs.

I've never seen such a breathtaking view. Ocean and beach as far as I can see, with the last remnants of beach-goers dotting the sand as they gather their beach towels and chairs and wrangle their children. Endless palm trees and green grass, basketball courts and people on roller-skates and skateboards.

The patio we're currently sitting on is filled with outdoor couches and tables, with small fireplaces scattered around, creating an intimate setting for a date.

And I can't help the jump that my heart does every time he looks at me.

Jeremy.

This hot-as-sin man is very quickly becoming some-one I want to spend more time with. I've never had a boy-friend before – not that Jeremy would be my boyfriend – but I've always wondered what it would be like. I used to play it down in my head. Why just have the attention of one man when you can have the attention of many? It's an adrenaline rush for sure.

But nothing compared to how I feel when he looks at

me.

And I'm one hundred percent okay with it.

"So, the original plan was dinner here, but I think you're feeling a bit self conscious about how we're dressed," he says, tugging lightly on my still-damp ponytail. "So I thought we could watch the sunset here, which should be in about," he glances at his phone, "fifteen minutes." He leans forward and drops his phone on the table in front of us, then settles back against the couch. There's a big pause, before he adds, "Then maybe we can grab some take-out and head to the next place?"

"Next place?" I ask. When he only nods, I add, "How many phases are there to this date?"

"Awww, pretty girl. You trying to get rid of me?" he asks, smiling. But if I'm totally honest, he looks a little bewildered.

I can't help my own crooked grin. "I'm having too good of a time to call it a night, mister. I just wish I had more comfortable shoes on. And that my underwear wasn't damp and slowly seeping through the butt of these sweats."

He laughs, rubbing his free hand against his face. "I'm never gonna live it down, huh?"

I shake my head. "Not ever. A Davenport never goes out looking anything but perfect."

I immediately regret it as soon as I let it slip, especially when Jeremy gives me a confused expression.

I wave my hand in front of me to say it's no big deal. "Just my mother's thought process. She's quite the darling in our little town. Always so put together. It's why I'm enjoying the freedom of college so much," I finish with a laugh.

"She sounds… interesting," he finally says, and I laugh again at his choice of word to describe my mother.

"Interesting is one way to put it," I say, leaning forward to take a sip of my soda. "I like to use the term 'indefinitely disappointed.' I mean, she has her good points too. She was really supportive about the things that made sense to her. She grew up in a really stuffy household – like, when we visited her parents in Connecticut, we weren't allowed to touch *anything*. I don't think she imagined a life where she ended up in Nebraska, so she does everything she can to make her life in Kilburn feel like it did growing up."

"Can someone actually make Nebraska feel like growing up in Connecticut?" he asks with a twinkle in his eyes.

"I know. It sounds ridiculous, but it's just her way to cope. I guess marrying my dad was her one act of rebellion, even though he wasn't some schmuck. But she came from Old Money, and my dad was definitely a New Money guy, which her parents didn't approve of. My brother and sister and I didn't even meet our grandparents until we were like, in elementary school because they weren't talking to my mom for a long time. They weren't even invited to her wedding. And then when we finally did meet them, she was *so different*. She's never been a really demonstrative person, but it was like going back to her parents' house and having their eyes on her made her shut off any ability to feel empathy."

I shrug, taking my eyes away from Jeremy to glance down at the boardwalk.

"As we got older, she became more and more strict about what we were and weren't allowed to do. And it was all very rigid. Like, my brother was expected to do things that were athletic, but nothing too brutish. Running, golf, tennis, swimming. My sister and I both had piano lessons until we were in high school, and if we'd wanted to, we could have taken ballet or joined book clubs or volunteered for charities."

Jeremy laughs.

"I know, right? Like, what century do we live in? This isn't *Pride and Prejudice* and I wasn't trying to do anything totally off the wall. I wanted to play volleyball and join the Pre-Med club in high school, not snort cocaine." I laugh. "But that's what I mean. I stuck with the piano lessons and did dance recitals each year until I was almost sixteen, and my mom was so encouraging and supportive. She was at every show and drove me to all my practices. She smiled more and told me she was proud of me."

I shake my head. "But whenever I would ask to do something that didn't align with what *she* wanted for me, she was like a completely different person, you know? And my dad... I think he's just so in love with my mom and so worried that she'll leave to go back to her old life that he lets her do whatever, even if it's stifling for his kids or even himself."

I let my eyes wander over the people walking past us in bright colors and bathing suits. "I've wondered a few times who he used to be – before my mom got so straight laced, if that time even exists."

I turn to Jeremy with a smile. "I found this photo album once of the two of them from the 80s. My dad had this super sweet red car and my mom had this big wild hair and a mini dress. I almost died when I found it. It's full of photos of these two people I feel like I've never met before."

"That's kind of sad, when you put it that way,' he says, squeezing my hand slightly.

I nod. "I know. But I can't force them to be who they were in their twenties, you know? Just like I don't want them trying to force me to be someone I'm not."

When I look up at Jeremy, I see a soft smile playing on his face. "What?" I ask.

He shrugs. "You're just really mature," he says with a half laugh. "I don't know, I guess when I think about my asshole dad I only think about what I can change about him. I've never really thought about anything positive." He shrugs again and shakes his head just slightly. "I don't know."

We slip into a comfortable silence and keep our eyes focused on the horizon as the sun starts to dip low in the sky. The sunsets on the coast are so different than at home. Nebraska sunsets are majestic, with the sun shining out from behind clouds, beams of light breaking through wisps of white in ethereal rays that hint at a higher being sitting just beyond them.

The sunset tonight looks like it could set the world on fire. Hot pinks and violent orange streaks the sky, the color only broken up by the palm trees that look black against the brightness of the sun in the distance.

"Looks like fire, doesn't it?" Jeremy asks.

I nod, not taking my eyes off of the sun, even though it hurts my eyes. "I was just thinking that. It's so harsh, it makes everything look like a photo that's been sun-bleached. But there's a strange vibrancy to it too. It's different than anything I've seen before. I don't really know how it makes me feel, but I know I like it."

When I finally take my eyes off of the sun and glance

at Jeremy, I find him staring at me.

"I know what you mean," he says, his voice low. And I know he's not talking about the sunset.

I give him a shy smile and lean further into him, kissing him lightly on the neck before forcing myself to look back at the gorgeous view as the sun finally starts to break across the horizon.

"You know about the green flash?" Jeremy says, and I shake my head.

"Never heard of it."

"Well, there are lots of legends about it, and there are legit scientific explanations too. But my favorite is in the Jimmy Buffett song."

"Who's Jimmy Buffett?" I ask.

His mouth opens slightly then he laughs. "Okay, we will revisit this conversation, definitely. But Jimmy wrote a short song called *Green Flash at Sunset*. It's not on any albums, it's just something I stumbled across one day online."

He reaches forward and grabs his phone again, flipping through and pulling something up online. A slow acoustic song starts up, and he holds his phone up between us so I can hear the words.

I listen for about forty seconds, and then it's over.

"I think that's the shortest song I've ever heard," I say, feeling a little confused by the lyrics. "What does it mean?"

"It's essentially saying that the green flash is an illusion, like recapturing young love, something we wish was there but isn't real."

"Well, *that's* depressing," I reply.

Jeremy smiles, but there's a sadness there now. "That's

life sometimes, right?" I nod. "Let's watch for it. I've only seen it a few times."

I turn my eyes back towards the setting sun, which is now over halfway sunken in the horizon. It suddenly becomes very important to see the green flash, even if it *is* an illusion. Because what is life if you can't hope to see something special. My eyes burn when I focus hard on the sun as it continues to dip in the sky.

And just as the last little bits disappear, I lean forward and...

Nothing.

"Did you see anything?" I ask him, sure that my tired eyes must have missed it.

"Nope. Not today," he replies. "But that's the great thing about living so close to the coast," he says as he stands and tugs me up behind him. "Every day is a new chance."

I smile up at him, happy to see that the sadness in his eyes is gone. "That's a pretty romantic concept, Mister Jameson. I didn't think you had it in you."

He smirks, his playful side reappearing suddenly. "You have no idea what I'm capable of, pretty girl."

An hour later, we're sitting in light traffic, destination unknown, at least to me. After wrapping up the sunset, we walked back to Jeremy's car and took a little detour through McDonalds. He was a little surprised when I ordered a triple cheeseburger and large fries. I just shrugged. I plan to take advantage of my ridiculously fast metabolism while I can.

"So where is this mysterious part two?" I ask as I take another huge bite of my cheeseburger and groan. "Seriously, I know this is made up of like, body parts, but it's so. Dang. Good."

Jeremy laughs and I chuck a fry at him.

"Well, we've got a few options," he says, flicking his blinker and changing lanes.

"Oooooh, I like options. Hit me."

"Well, first, we could go where I had originally planned, which is up into the mountains. September is a great month to possibly see meteor showers, but there's too much light pollution in the city to see them."

"Okay, stargazing. What else?"

"There's a drive-in movie theatre in Alhambra that does 9pm showings."

"Oh that sounds awesome," I say, balling up the wrapper and shoving it into the paper bag.

"Or, we could head back to my place, and you could change. And we could watch a movie there." He says this last option almost reluctantly. Which doesn't make sense to me.

"Mister Jameson," I say, flirtatiously. "After all your showboating and innuendo yesterday about having a *good time* tonight, are you a little shy about the idea of taking me home?"

He laughs, a little self-consciously. "Well, I just…" he clears his throat. "I'm having a great time tonight, and to be honest, Charlie, I would love nothing more than to take you home." He puffs out a breath. "But I'm also okay if that doesn't happen."

He eyes me briefly before turning his attention back to the road. "We can do any of these things another time, or we can do them tonight. Completely up to you."

Another time.

This whole date, I've been fighting internally with myself. His actions have been screaming that this isn't a one-time deal. But his reputation is also fairly loud, and I haven't been able to help the second-guessing, knowing that this was likely going to be a one and done. And I was okay with that. Earlier. I really was.

But I'm not anymore. This man has been sliding stealthily beneath my skin. The flirtation is heart-racing, but the sincerity and genuine interest is enough to prickle the backs of my eyes.

So now, I have to decide what I want.

Am I ready for whatever happens tonight if I go home with him?

I take him in where he sits behind the wheel, the lights from the highway passing us by in waves, his face going in and out of shadow. He's so handsome. But what really makes me want to be around him is that good heart of his. The one that makes him look unsure sometimes. The one that loves and protects his sister.

And I know without a doubt that no matter what happens between us in the future, I want to go all in with him tonight.

I lean across the center console and place a soft kiss to his neck, just below his jaw.

"Take me home," I whisper.

I see him swallow. I've clearly taken him by surprise.

And I like that.

When I sit back in my seat, he reaches over and loops his hand with mine, slowly stroking the skin on my palm, running his fingers softly between the dips and valleys of mine. On the surface, it's a fairly innocent sign of affection, but it's causing my skin to boil, a heat rushing up my chest and flushing at my neck.

We ride the rest of the way to Jeremy's that way, our hands together apart from a few times he uses both hands at the wheel. And by the time we pull into the parking lot of his apartment complex, I'm a bundle of nerves.

When we walk through his front door and he flips on the lights, I take a moment to survey his home. It makes me want to laugh a bit, which is a nice feeling that helps curb my slightly erratic nervousness. He's in that zone between college student and adult. A fancy TV on a shitty stand. A nice couch with laundry dumped on it. His kitchen is the same, with red solo cups stacked up underneath hanging wine glasses and next to a decanter. It's like his apartment is going through puberty.

"What's so funny?" he asks as he toes off his shoes at the door and takes my purse to set it on the small table near the entry.

"Just super impressed at your ability to pull off the 'I'm in college but I'm also a real adult' style." He looks a bit confused, so I dive into my explanation, pointing things out to him. "I'm not making fun, I promise," I try to reassure him when he looks a bit unsure. "I can see that you're really comfortable here, which is more than I can say about anywhere I've ever lived. It's just so clear that you're trying to be an adult, and it just makes me feel so young. That's all."

His shoulders relax and he gives me a small smile. "Glad to know you approve of my latest art installation. I like to call it *Unfinished Business*," he says, gesturing to the laundry pile.

I crack up as he walks to the pile and lifts it all into his arms, carrying it down a short hallway to what I can only guess is his bedroom.

When he returns, he has a towel, a shirt and some boxers in hand. "I figured you'd want to shower off, and then we can watch a movie or something." He motions towards the bathroom, which sits across from his bedroom. "I'll just put these in here."

I walk past him and into the small room, turning to thank him before closing the door. After a good rinse and scrub to get off all the sand and salt, I dry off and pull on Jeremy's clothes, giving them a slight sniff. They smell like him and I love being enveloped in that clean, earthy smell. When I walk back out to the living room, I find Jeremy on the couch, surfing through the TV channels.

"Better?" he asks when I plop down next to him.

"Much," I respond. "Except I'm all pruney." I lift my foot just slightly in front of me, showcasing my super wrinkly toes. "I don't think my toesies were a fan of being wet and shoved into boots all evening," I say with a laugh.

Jeremy laughs too. "Don't worry. Pruney or not, your *toesies* are still adorable." He stands and hands me the remote. "I'm gonna shower, then I'll be back. Feel free to pick a movie you want to watch. I have Netflix."

"Sweet!" I reply as he heads to the bathroom to clean up.

I spend a few minutes flicking through the options and finally settle on *Die Hard*. Can't go wrong with an action movie, I'm sure.

When Jeremy finally comes out of the bathroom, I feel my throat dry up and my eyes go wide. He's got on a pair of plaid pajama pants and a light blue shirt that makes his eyes bright. I don't know why I'm reacting to him like this, with my skin getting clammy and my heart starting to thump a bit more aggressively. It's not like he's doing a strip tease or something. He's literally just coming into the living room in a pair of modest pajamas.

He drops down on the couch next to me.

"Oh, *Die Hard*. Always a good choice," he says, clicking the play button. He settles in and glances over at me, where I sit like a rigid board. "You okay?" he asks.

I nod, not saying anything, then try to force myself to settle and get comfortable. Jeremy lifts his arm and motions for me to snuggle in next to him. So I do.

The minute I'm pressed up against him and I smell that delicious soapy smell wafting off of his still warm skin, the nervousness begins to melt away.

I rest my hand on his stomach as the movie begins, playing lightly with the material of his shirt. After a few minutes, his free hand joins mine, and he starts with the torturous finger touching again. Heat creeps along my skin, and my breathing becomes a bit harsh. And then, almost without my permission, my hand slides under his shirt just slightly, my thumb softly stroking the skin beneath. Jeremy stills for just a second, but I can hear his heart beating in his chest, his steady thump picking up speed, his own breathing becoming a bit rougher in my ear.

When I finally have the nerve to look up at him, he looks at me for only a second before his lips are on mine, his tongue plunging in as if he wants to suck the air out of my chest. I can't do anything but moan and grip him harder, my fingers pressing deeper into his flesh. He raises slightly and pushes me onto my back on the couch, leaning over me and continuing to kiss while his hands roam across my body. My hips, my thighs, tilting my leg up and pressing against me where my legs split, eliciting another moan from deep in my chest.

"Jeremy," I whisper.

He pulls back and looks at me, panting slightly. "You okay?" he asks.

I nod. "I just…" I pause.

"Whatever it is, it's okay," he says back.

"Okay, well. I just, I don't know if I'm ready for… you know. It's just a little fast. I didn't want to spoil the mood, but I just wanted to tell you now so you weren't expecting it."

Jeremy smiles at me, a warm smile that melts my insides and pushes my fears aside. "Hey, I don't expect anything from you, pretty girl." He starts to pull away, but I grip him and hold him close to me.

"I'm… I'm okay with what we're doing now, though," I whisper, squirming slightly at the ache that throbs low, where he rests against me. "Can we…"

His smile turns lustful and he bites his lip, pressing harder against me where he rests between my legs. He closes his eyes in pleasure as he grinds into me, but I can't look away from his strong jaw and the look of bliss that has overtaken his expression.

"Like this?" he asks, leaning forward and pressing his lips to my neck, temporarily drawing my focus to the area he's licking and sucking, biting slightly. "This what you want?" he whispers into my ear, then rolls his hips.

I whimper, unable to contain the feelings that are rushing through my body. "Yes," I say back.

"Good. I only ever want to make you feel good," he

responds, pressing his lips back against mine. I twist my arms around his neck, holding him to me, and give in to the desire I'm feeling.

It's hot and heavy, and the time passes so quickly, we don't even notice when the credits on the TV begin to roll.

CHAPTER SIX
Charlie

September
Five Years Ago

The first thing I notice is the sunlight. I have blackout curtains in my room on campus, so all of this blaring sun isn't right. I roll over and see Jeremy, asleep, naked. His strong shoulders and back awash with light from the window, allowing me to see all of the tiny hairs on his body.

I snuggle closer to him, happy to be the 'big spoon', and rest my face against his back, breathing him in. I love this, the quiet intimacy of waking first. And if I'm honest with myself, I'm thankful I have a few minutes to process last night without Jeremy's inspection or potential questions.

So…. I had sex.

I giggle softly and press a kiss to Jeremy's back.

It hadn't been the plan. Jeremy had called it quits on the couch last night due to things getting too… hard?

I giggle again.

He invited me to stay the night. We snuggled up in

his bed and fell asleep. Or at least, Jeremy did. I stayed awake for a while, playing over the pros and cons to sleeping with him. The first time I would ever have sex with someone.

And I came to the realization that not everyone gets a special first time. Something to remember. And I knew that no matter what happened with Jeremy, it would always be special.

My face flushes red in embarrassment at remembering my boldness. I'd softly woken him with kisses and light strokes across his stomach.

"Jeremy," I'd whispered. "Make love to me."

Now, in the light of yesterday's choices, I squirm a bit, worrying that I came across too aggressive. But I shake it off. I shouldn't feel apologetic for the sexual desires my body has. That's just Feminism 101.

And he didn't seem to mind last night. "Are you sure you want to?" he'd whispered back, almost like he didn't want to break whatever spell I was under.

"Yes," I replied. "I want you."

He gave me this soft grin, the light from the street lamp outside making his eyes bright. His hands trembled as we removed our clothes, but became confident and assured once we were pressed together, the pleasure of being so connected overshadowing the pain of my first time.

And when we came apart, it took everything inside of me to keep from crying at the depth of feeling that was soaring through my body, from the tips of my toes to the ends of each strand of hair.

I thought it couldn't get any better, but then Jeremy held me close until I fell asleep, stroking my back, his hands in my hair.

Light murmuring from Jeremy draws me back to
the now, to this room where we both lie naked in bed,
wrapped together.

"Morning," I hear from him, and he gives the hand
that rests on his stomach a light squeeze. He rolls over
and looks at me with a crooked smile, something soft and
genuine that somehow keeps me from responding. So I
just lean forward and kiss his jaw.

"Morning," I finally manage on a whisper.

Jeremy tries to kiss me on the mouth, but I pull away.

"I haven't brushed my teeth," I say.

"I don't care," he replies, coming back at me and kissing me deep, deep, sweet and sexy.

When he finally pulls away, my eyelids flutter open to
find him out of bed and tugging on some pants.

"What sounds good for breakfast?" he asks, yanking a
shirt from his clean clothes pile at the foot of his dresser.

"Whatever is fine," I reply, sitting up and holding the
sheet against my chest. "But you don't have to make me
breakfast. I can grab something later."

He rests his elbow against his dresser. "You have somewhere to be today?"

I nod. "I'm supposed to visit my Nan for lunch. Do
you know what time it is?"

He grabs his phone. "It's almost ten."

"Yeah, I should get home and get ready. I can just
grab a muffin or something on campus," I say, slipping
out of the bed with the sheet still wrapped around me.

"Hey," he says softly, reaching for me and tugging
me close before I can do anything about it. He pulls my
hair to the side and twists it lightly in his hand. "I'm not
trying to hint for you to get out or anything like that. You

know that, right?"

I rock up onto my toes and press my lips to his. When I drop back down, I smile. "I definitely know that. I just really do have plans today and I wasn't..." I glance down at my sheet covered body then look back up at him with a smirk, "... I wasn't exactly expecting to spend the night. So I'm feeling a little flustered and just need to get home to get ready and go see my Nan."

The tiny wrinkles between his brow smooth out at my response. He places a quick kiss on my lips, then spins me and slaps my buns through the sheet. "Get dressed, pretty girl, and I'll get you back to campus."

Twenty minutes later, Jeremy pulls up to the front of Eidelman and puts his car in park. The campus is always dead on Saturday mornings, and I'm thankful no one will be around to see me hauling up to my room in the sweats and t-shirt I'm wearing that clearly belong to someone else. I don't necessarily believe in *the walk of shame* – basically because I don't think any woman should feel ashamed after hooking up – but the last thing I want is for RJ to realize I was out all night with her brother. And it would be just my luck if she popped out of those doors right now.

"I had a great time last night," Jeremy says, interrupting my thoughts.

I smile at him and rest my head back against the seat, turning slightly sideways to take him in. "Me too."

His eyes search my face.

"Well, I'd better..."

"Did you want to…"

We both laugh.

"You go first," I say.

Jeremy clears his throat. "I'm still down to go stargazing tonight if you want to. Or we can hit up the drive in movie. Just shoot me a text when you're done."

The smile on my face is ridiculous. I tuck my hair behind my ears.

"As much as I would love that, I have my very first college presentation on Monday and I haven't even started it," I say with a laugh. "Can we do something this week? My schedule is pretty open after Monday."

He looks happy with my response and promises to call me later today or tomorrow to get it scheduled.

After a searing kiss, I hop out of the car, and jog up the steps to Eidelman, unable to contain the glee. When I get to the top, I turn to wave goodbye and find him staring at me with the window down.

"Have a good day, pretty girl," he says, then drives off.

I spin on my heels and race to the elevator, giddy with excitement. I don't know *how* I'm going to focus on this stupid presentation when all I want to do is gush to everyone I know about my date with Jeremy.

But my excitement sobers up when I realize that the one person I want to share with is his sister. RJ is *not* going to want to talk about my first time having sex if she realizes it's her brother.

I let out a groan. Sometimes, secrets can be fun, like sneaking makeup books home during high school. But this is definitely not one of those times. As the elevator doors close and I ascend to my floor, I wonder how I'm going to keep RJ from realizing what happened.

CHAPTER SEVEN
Jeremy

September
Five Years Ago

I love college. Even though I think bigger and better things are coming soon, I'm a little sad that my time at Glendale is coming to an end this year. I basically get paid to play the sport I love, and I still get to enjoy parties and hanging out with friends and, of course, the women.

Glendale College was my only choice. I had a few options on the table, including heading to the Midwest to play soccer with a friend of mine at a pretty well-known state school that has a few National Championship titles already. But when I thought about it, I wanted to be the big fish in a small pond. I'd spent enough of my life being the small fish at home, and I wasn't about to repeat that if I didn't absolutely have to.

"Hey, Jeremy!" I hear from my left. I turn and give a little wave to the group of girls sitting together, smiles huge on their faces as they eat their salads and bags of veggies.

I appreciate eating healthy – you have to find value in nutrition when your world revolves around your body's ability to do what you want it to do – but man did I also appreciate Charlie's ability to wolf down that big ass burger this weekend. I laugh just thinking about the absolutely massive bites she was taking.

I plop my butt down at an empty table, the same one my sister and I sit at every Monday for lunch, and rip open the sandwich I got from the sub shop on campus. Sometimes I stand in line in the Caf with Rachel and just grab whatever is available, but I'm not the one forced to be on a meal plan, and I just can't stomach that cafeteria crap today.

But before I take a bite, my phone dings with an alert. Digging it out of my pocket, I smile when I see it's from Charlie.

Charlotte (Rachel's Hot Roommate): Yes!
Let's definitely hit up the drive-in tonight.
SO STOKED.

Me: You should be. They're playing Die
Hard. I figure we didn't really watch it last
*time, so we could try again. *wink**

*Charlotte (Rachel's Hot Roommate): *blush**
Yeah, we were a little preoccupied. Although
looking back, I think watching Die Hard
would have been more interesting.

I hit call the second I receive her text. It rings twice before she answers, and all I hear is laughter, which makes me smile.

"You think the movie would have been more interesting, huh?" I ask with a smile, knowing she's just going to continue to laugh.

"Maybe," she says, stretching out the word, then laughing again.

"You're pretty cute, you know that, right?"

Her laughter fades off, but I can hear the smile in her voice when she just says "uh huh."

"What time should I pick you up tonight? You wanna grab dinner first or should we pack a bag of goodies to take with us?"

"Ooooh!" she shouts into the phone. "Definitely a bag of goodies. I'll take care of that. I know *exactly* what to bring."

"Alright, well I'll pick you up at six, then. Sound good?"

"Yeah it does," she replies. She pauses. "I'm really looking forward to spending some more time with you, Jeremy."

My stomach tightens in the best way, and I can't help the smile that stretches across my face. I'm pretty sure I look like a clown.

"Alright, pretty girl. See you tonight."

I stare at my phone once we've hung up. This is… different. But, good different. I think. I can't remember the last time I went on a second date. It's definitely not happened in college, I can say that for certain. But I'm just… I can't wait to hear her laugh again.

My good mood continues to grow when Rachel plops down next to me and I see the gross shit in her to-go container from the Caf. Thank sweet baby Jesus I grabbed a sandwich today.

"Hey dude," she says, before shoveling some potato into her mouth. "What's up?"

I laugh. "You know the shit they serve in the Caf is going to give you cancer, right?"

She just takes another monster bite and lifts her middle finger at me.

"Not all of us have the option of choosing whatever food we want, mister," she finally says once she's swallowed her bite of the chalkiest looking potato I've ever seen.

I roll my eyes. "I'd buy you lunch if you'd let me. We both know I have more money than you, and will likely *always* have more money than you once I go pro. So just *give in*, baby sister. Let me buy you something that doesn't look like it came out of someone's butt."

She laughs. "*Fine*," she says on a sigh. "I give in. Moving forward, just bring me something to eat on Mondays. Or maybe we could try eating off-campus."

I nod. "Finally, you see my wisdom."

We spend the next twenty or so minutes catching up on how school and soccer have been for both of us. Rachel is about two months in to playing for the women's team here at Glendale, and she's really enjoying it so far. But there's some bitch on the team that gives her sass all the time. After she's done complaining about one of her teammates, I decide to dip my toe into the water.

"So, how's that roommate of yours doing? She get up to anything fun this weekend?" I ask.

Rachel always gets mad when I hook up with people she knows, and being an awesome big brother, sometimes I like to tease her a little. But this time, I want to test the waters and see how she'd feel about me and Charlie. Because if my instincts are correct, this very well could turn into something.

Which is why I'm shocked at the barely controlled disgust I see morphing on her face.

"You're a twenty-one-year-old senior in college," she growls. "What? You've already stuck your dick in everyone your own age and have to move on to the barely legal? You're so gross." My mouth drops open and I scoff, preparing a response when she comes at me again, jabbing a finger into my chest. "You should be embarrassed that you have to troll for freshmen to get laid."

"Hey, I can't help it if I appeal to everyone," I say with a shrug. But really, what am I supposed to say?

We've already done the deed, so you can't be mad.

Yeah, I'm sure that will go over really well. "Besides, Charlie didn't seem to have an issue with me."

Rachel's eyes narrow and I see her wheels turning. "She is completely off-limits."

I just smirk at her. When has anyone ever been off-limits? That's ridiculous.

"I'm serious Jer!" she cries out. "You've fucked and chucked enough girls this year. Leave. Her. Alone."

I frown at her. "Hey, I don't fuck and chuck, Rachel. That implication about my character is just rude. I'm offended."

But she's not done.

"Oh really? So Andi, Rebecca, Jennifer… they were serious girlfriends?"

I hide my smile as I remember the gorgeous seniors from Rachel's soccer team. Yeah, they were still in high school, but I was twenty and they were eighteen and having fun on spring break. *Sue me.*

"You can't pull out one example of exercising my right to get in some physical exercise from over a year ago and make it sound like that's how I live my entire life, Rach."

I pause trying to sound sincere without being obvious. "What if I really like Charlie? I can do the whole... dating thing."

But she just closes her eyes and sighs, rubbing the bridge of her nose like I'm causing her all kinds of problems.

"Jer, you know I have a hard time making friends. Charlie and I get along really well, and I don't want anything to ruin that."

Then she looks me right in the face with eyes that are so sincere, and a little bit sad, and I know I'm going to hate what she says next.

"Please. I am *begging* you. Turn your penis off for one minute and do your lonely, friendless sister a solid. Pretend. Charlie. Doesn't. Exist."

My stomach tightens again, but this time in discomfort.

Figures.

The first time I feel a real connection with someone, something deep and light at the same time, and it becomes something off-limits.

But what am I supposed to do? Tell my sister that I've already taken Charlie on a date? Let her know that both of us technically snuck around behind her back? I can't promise her that things with Charlie will last – hell, I can barely plan out my week, let alone try to decide what things will look like in a few months.

So what can I do except agree?

I look back at Rachel, who looks so desperate to keep this friendship, and I let out a resigned breath.

"You have my word. From here on out, Charlie doesn't exist."

She lets out a sigh of relief and tilts her head back, whispering, "Thankyouthankyouthankyou."

I smile a little, glad I was able to make my sister happy. But the smile isn't completely genuine, since that pit in my stomach keeps growing.

And I can't help but wonder if I've done the right thing.

CHAPTER EIGHT
Charlie

September
Five Years Ago

When I see Jeremy waiting at the curb for me in his car, I can't help the giddy energy that rips through my entire body. It's only been a few days since our first date, but I can't *wait* for date number two.

I practically skip down the steps and pull the door open, smiling at him as I plop into the passenger seat.

"I am *so* excited, Jeremy, literally I've never been to a drive in movie before and it always seems like the greatest thing in the world," I say as I tug my seatbelt on and start rummaging through my bag.

"Okay, so, I didn't have a lot of time to get all of this shit together, so you'll have to forgive me for how lame it us. However," I pull out a bottle of vodka, "I *did* manage to sneak this out of my friend's room while she was taking a test. Maybe it makes me a thief, but I figure she's basically an alcoholic anyway and will find a way to get some more." I shrug. "That, or I'll have you help me buy a replacement bottle some other day. But, let's be honest, Kendra does *not* need any more alcohol after that incident with the lawnmower that RJ told me about."

I lean forward and lower my voice. "Apparently she cut the grass on the quad in the shape of a giant penis, which, if you really think about it, is impressive considering how drunk she was at the time," I say with a laugh.

But Jeremy doesn't laugh. He gives me a slightly pained smile and a nod.

"What's wrong?" I ask, suddenly concerned, the smile falling from my face. "Is everything okay?"

"Yeah. Well…" he lets out a sigh. "Actually no, not everything is okay."

I turn to face him. "If it's about me stealing the alcohol I can totally go put it back. I'm not *actually* a thief," I say, unsure if something's wrong with what I've said or something else entirely.

"Listen, Charlie…"

And…my stomach plummets.

"I had an amazing time with you this weekend. Like, a really great time. But I think this may have moved too quickly, you know?"

I think I nod, the acid in my stomach rolling around and making me feel queasy.

"I figured, you know, we'd grab a bite, have some fun… nothing serious. And I had a really great time with you. Really."

"Uh huh," I say, not looking at him anymore, just staring vacantly at the stupid bottle of Vodka in my hands.

I can't believe I did this. I can't *believe* I slept with him this weekend and then thought something would come from it. Like he's some guy who really wants to get into a relationship when that's not at all who he is. RJ warned me about this, didn't she? Didn't she tell me that every girl he takes out is shocked when things don't go somewhere serious, even when he makes it clear that's not what he wants?

And apparently I'm one of them.

I let out a controlled breath through my pursed lips, talking myself down, trying to remind myself that I didn't sleep with Jeremy because I was in love with him, or because he promised me something, or because I thought we were going to start dating.

I did it because I was ready, and because I wanted to have my first sexual experience be with someone I enjoyed spending time with, as opposed to some awkward and uncomfortable mistake like so many others' first times.

"But anything more than just a good time is... well, I don't know that it's in the cards for me," he says.

He takes a breath like he's gearing up for another round of *it's not you, it's me,* but I put my hand on his arm to stop him. I even manage to smile, even though it's taking every ounce of energy in my body to keep from breaking down into tears.

"Hey, it's okay, Jeremy. No big deal."

He stares at me.

"You're okay?"

I nod, my lips tucked into my mouth. I start shoving everything back into my bag.

"Don't worry about me, mister," I say. "I knew what I was getting myself into when I said I'd go out with you. I guess I just got a little ahead of myself, but..." I choke a little bit on my words. "Like I said, don't worry. We both got what we originally wanted out of our date. I got a great night out and to see the beach and talk to someone other than my roommate, and you got..." I glance at him, then flush slightly but refuse to look away, "... well, you got what you wanted too."

Jeremy looks startled by what I've said. He curses and runs his hand through his hair.

"Charlie, come on, you have to know..."

"I had a great time getting to know you a little bit," I say, cutting him off. I don't want to hear excuses. Instead, I reach over and press my hand to his chest, over his heart. "You might think you're not a relationship person, but I believe you have a good heart. Don't keep it away from finding the right person."

I lean in and kiss his cheek, then open the car door and get out, lugging my bag over my shoulder.

"Bye Jeremy," I say, and shut the door, then walk as confidently as I can back into my building, knowing his eyes are probably still on me.

I make it through the doors, up the elevator, and all the way to my room before the tears start to fall.

A few hours later, I get a text message. I roll over in bed, grabbing my phone and squinting through my puffy eyes.

> *Jeremy: Look, can we agree that Rachel doesn't need to know about this? I just want to make sure things aren't weird.*

Prick.

Part of me wants to tell Rachel so Jeremy can get the ass-chewing of his life. But I'm a little embarrassed that Rachel told me not to mess around with Jeremy and I did it anyway. She's best-friend material, something hard to come by. And I don't want to fuck it up.

Me: Don't worry. It never happened.

I never get a response.

CHAPTER NINE
Jeremy

January
Present Day

I turn in my seat as a hand rests softly on my shoulder. The blonde with a sweet smile is someone I would normally be happy about approaching me.

But not tonight.

"Wanna buy me a drink?" she asks, taking a seat on the stool next to mine.

Part of me wants to say yes, to get myself out of this funk I've been in. It's been months of the same thing. I spend the normal part of my life doing what I should be doing: working out, going to practice, spending time with my sister – although that quality time has dropped off a bit since she officially started dating her guy. Then when the day is over, I get a drink.

I used go to a shithole near my place. At first, it was fairly anonymous, but when you spend enough time in a place, people feel like they know you. They ask questions and want to chitchat.

I don't drink anymore to make small talk. I don't actually know why I do it anymore, but it's definitely not for that reason.

So, for the past few weeks I've been going to a bar near my sister's place. O'Reilly's. It's not anywhere near my house, but it's walking distance from hers. She doesn't need to know that I've been sleeping it off in my truck parked down the street from her apartment complex. It's a thirty-minute drive from the area I live in, but I like it.

You'd think with not wanting to chat, I would go to some beat down place. But I've found that it's better to go somewhere busy. Sure, every so often someone comes along and wants to start something up – like the blonde next to me that's currently waving down the bartender – but for the most part, at college bars like this one, everyone is here to meet up with people they already know. And that means I get to sit at the bar and drink without being bothered, apart from the bartender asking if I want another.

The blonde asks for a chardonnay, then turns and smiles at me again.

She's cute, and some other night, I'd be lucky to have her sit down next to me and strike up a conversation. Maybe take her home. But tonight isn't that night. I haven't had a night where that felt right for months.

"Look," I say, just as she opens her mouth to speak. "I'm not really in the mood for talking."

I expect the look on her face to fall slightly or for her to tell me to fuck off and pretend like all she wanted was a free drink.

Which is why my mind is blown when her smile widens into something a little less sweet and a little more wicked.

"Me neither," she says, leaning closer. "So why don't we skip the foreplay and just jump right to the good stuff."

My mouth nearly drops open, but I'm just wasted enough to laugh. Which I'm guessing is not the response she was hoping for, judging by the way her head jerks back and her smile falls away to reveal a slightly affronted look.

"I appreciate the offer," I respond, grabbing my glass off the bar and swallowing the rest in one go. I huff out a breath in reaction to how it hits me. When did I switch to whiskey? "But that's not what I meant," I say.

I pull out my wallet and shuffle through the bills, not seeing super clearly. I grab a wad and chuck it down on the bar with a nod to the bartender. "I'm saying I'm not interested. Not tonight."

Her face wipes completely blank when she realizes I'm not biting.

"Night, ma'am," I say as I turn and half-walk, half-stumble away from her.

The last thing I hear as I head towards the door is, "Did he just call me *ma'am?*"

When I take a step outside, I breathe in deeply, letting the cool January air into my lungs. January in Southern California is a weird time. The temperature around Christmas is usually in the seventies, and then almost as soon as the new year hits, the evening temps plummet, sometimes getting as cool as the mid thirties. It's a novelty to a lot of people when their lawns get a bit of frost on them overnight, but I think it's a nuisance. I've never liked cold weather, and January is my least favorite month. It means when I wake up to go to the gym in the morning, I'll be freezing my nuts off.

Tonight is a night like that, and I don't look forward to what's ahead. I flip my phone out and check the temperature, shocked when I see it's dipped to twenty-eight degrees. Well, tonight is officially going to be a nasty night to try to sleep this shit off in my car.

I start the few block walk to where my SUV is parked near Rachel's apartment. It's a pretty decent neighborhood, and at only just past midnight on a weekend, there are still quite a few people out and about.

It doesn't take long for me to make it to my car. I unlock it and climb in, turning the ignition and immediately cranking the heat and turning on the seat warmers. The perks of signing a pro contract and getting a few marketing deals. I never would have been able to afford this SUV on my own. No job I ever could have gotten would have paid me enough for a car like this.

I lean the seat back and try to get comfortable, which is a tough thing to do when you're drunk and trying to fall asleep in a car, no matter how warm the seats are.

I rub my face with my hands.

I need to cut this shit out. Getting wasted at the bar. Alone.

Who does that remind you of?

I cringe.

It's no secret that my dad is a fucking mess. Especially not after he literally ran my sister over with his car last year. He's an abusive asshole who used to get an ego boost from smacking my sister around and treating her like general shit. I can't stand that I never knew about what was happening to her.

My mind rushes back to that day last year, when Rachel finally told me that my dad had been abusing her regularly during her final years of high school, after I left for college. I don't think I've ever cried like that before. The bastard smacked her around and I never knew. If I had, I would have gotten her out of that fucking house, that toxic place where she started to believe she was worthless.

I huff out a breath, squeezing my hands into fists with how angry I am. Then I force myself to release my hands.

I might be angry now, but a few drinks here and there doesn't mean I'm like him.

It doesn't.

I would *never* hit anyone, or try to step on others to make me feel better about my pathetic life. That's the Frank Jameson way of operation. Not the Jeremy Jameson way.

After everything that happened last year, Rachel and I confronted him. Go to rehab, or go to hell. Well, maybe it wasn't that nasty, but that was the basic gist of it. I was so proud of Rachel, standing up for herself. She told him she remembered when things were good when we were kids, and even though he didn't deserve her forgiveness, she realized that he was upset about our mom walking out and was taking it out on us. She forgave him.

To his *face*.

And then he basically spit on her and told her to fuck off. He didn't need rehab, he needed us to get out of his life.

So we did.

I've never seen Rachel cry that hard. She'd waited until we got into the car, leaving behind the house we grew up in for the last time. And then she broke down.

I didn't want her to cry. The guy was a bastard. We were both better off without him. So I told her that.

"I know," she said, tears streaming down her face. Even in her despair she tried to give me a small smile. "But there's this little part of me that always hoped he would change. You have to grieve when your hope dies, Jeremy. You have to mourn when you finally accept that something you've always wanted just isn't going to happen. Otherwise, you'll never move on from it."

So I'd let her cry her eyes out on the two-hour drive home. And when we got back to her apartment and Charlie came rushing out to her, holding her close as they walked inside together, I realized exactly what she meant. But for me, it wasn't about the man who let us down and pushed my sister around. It was the regret I felt, about the love I could have had, if I had just been strong enough.

That night in December was the first night I went out and got absolutely wasted. I figured the alcohol would help me mourn. Plenty of people drink their problems away, then wake up and start fresh. I'd never had a problem with drinking before.

Only, I did it the next night too. And the next. My thoughts about how screwed up my life was and the poor decisions I'd made, letting my sister down and ruining things with Charlie. They all stewed in my brain until I couldn't stand it anymore.

And then it was Christmas, and I had to sit across from Charlie at Rachel's family dinner. She always gives me this slightly pained smile, like she's happy I'm there because it makes Rachel happy, but if it was up to her she'd be nowhere near me. So I'd stepped out early because all I wanted was to go to the bar and not see her.

Now it's the day after New Years, and I'm drunk, nearly passed out in a car on the side of the road. Alone. And *still* thinking about Charlie.

I've had thoughts about her off and on over the years. That sweet laugh of hers kills me every time I hear it, although it doesn't happen as often when I'm around. She's gotten even more beautiful over the past three years, if that's even possible. But the thing that has been killing me the most is knowing that I had her, and made the choice to let her go.

I love my life – or, at least, I *did* love it – but I can't help but feel like I missed out on something beautiful. Something special. Something worth the care and time that a real relationship requires.

But there's nothing I can do about it now. She hates me, I'm sure. What else should she feel? From her vantage point, I pretended I was interested in something more than one date, took her virginity, and then showed her the door.

Too bad I can't let that little spark of hope die off, that maybe one day...

I shake myself, not wanting to get caught up in stupid hope.

I shift forward in the seat with a groan and turn off the engine now that my seat has warmed up enough to let me fall somewhat comfortably asleep. It'll be a bitch when I wake up cold in the morning, but I'm fine for now.

My eyes shoot open at the sound of a knock. It takes

me at least ten seconds of staring wide-eyed at Charlie through my car window before I remember where I am. And in those ten seconds, the reality of my current hangover smacks me in the face as my stomach rolls over.

Charlie looks at me with confused eyes, clearly wondering what I'm doing asleep and parked down the street from her and Rachel's apartment.

I rub my face with both hands, although the cold in the air is enough to wake me up. Turning on the car, I roll down the window.

Before I can even say a word, Charlie starts in.

"What the hell are you doing, Jeremy? How long have you been sleeping here? What is going on?"

Unbidden, my stomach rolls over again and I scramble out of the car. Bent over and bracing myself at the rear wheel, I heave up the acid that's been lurking in my stomach overnight. After a few seconds, I stand and lean against the SUV, resting my forehead on the cool window.

"Oh my god, are you okay?" Charlie asks, ever-the-nurse. She steps forward, completely disregarding the nasty shit all over the ground near my feet, and presses her hand to my cheek. "Are you sick?"

I turn to look at her and rest my cheek against the car, soaking in the cool feeling, my breath fogging the window as I take panting breaths.

"Don't worry about me. I'm fine," I finally manage. Which are not at all the words I actually wanted to say.

Charlie's face scrunches up like she's smelled something foul. "Are you...? Jeremy, are you *drunk?*"

I shake my head, then instantly regret it as another wave of nausea rolls through me.

"No, just... really hungover."

"Well you smell like the floor of a bar, and I've been in enough of them to promise you that's not a positive thing."

I give her a tight smile.

"What are you doing up so early?" I ask.

She shrugs. "Just running. I had some time to kill before my next shift starts, and I figured it was important to stick to my resolution of not being such a sloth when I'm not at work."

I let my eyes flick down her body, just now taking in her workout outfit. I don't know how I missed it. She's wearing red, black and gold Wonder Woman leggings, teal blue shoes, and a long-sleeved, neon yellow athletic shirt. The entire outfit is snug against her form, fitting to her every curve.

I look away before she catches me ogling her.

"I didn't know you ran," I say, pushing up from leaning on the car and tucking my hands in my pockets.

"There's a lot you don't know about me," she says.

I just nod, accepting the barb.

"Thanks for waking me up, Char. I gotta get going."

She takes a step away and watches me climb back into my car. When I pull away from the curb, she's still standing there, watching me. Her entire body is frowning at me, from her eyes to her mouth to the way she's standing with her arms crossed.

I hate that she saw that. But this is my reality.

And unfortunately, my reality gets even worse thirty minutes later. Three miles from my house, I notice the blue and reds flashing behind me.

Fuck.

CHAPTER TEN
Jeremy

January

"Jeremy Jameson."

My head flies up when my name is called. It takes a second for me to locate who's talking to me through the bars. The stress I've been feeling since making my phone call has been eating me alive. But when I spot the cop with the large waist, the ambivalence on his face reminds me that no one here cares about my personal problems.

"Ride's here."

I stand from where I'm seated on a long bench, surrounded by others in various stages of repose. I don't know why they seem so relaxed. I just want to shake them and say *you were arrested for something! How can you be so calm?*

I've only been arrested one other time – for beating up my sister's cheating high school boyfriend. Maybe I was calm then, because I knew I did what I needed to, and even today I know that I'd do it again. Maybe the people here aren't worried because they don't regret what they did to get here.

I can't say my time in the tank were particularly restful for me, though. I've been here for about four hours, practically climbing out of my skin, even though I'm sure I just looked like an angry drunk as I fumed in the corner. But what anyone on the outside looking in probably doesn't know is that I'm not angry at anyone but myself.

I follow the cop out to the front of the fairly small station. It's nothing like I remember, mostly because it was a different station I was booked in a few years ago. But also because I'm probably seeing it differently this time around.

When you're a sophomore in college who gives some cheating punk high-school prick a few pops to the face, when you're defending your family, the police station feels like something out of a movie. All grit and dark colors and gasping secretaries as you storm out after being released on your own recognizance. You're the superhero, the person being blamed for bringing down the hammer of rogue justice.

Now?

As a twenty-six-year-old professional soccer player that was pulled over for being over-the-limit at six o'clock in the morning?

It makes the lens through which I see the station cast a completely different light. It's a drab building with cracks in the walls and watermarks on the ceiling. Tan tables covered in paperwork, phones ringing, two people talking at a water cooler as they hold tiny white cups, with the smell of stale coffee in the air. And this time, when people look at me, I feel a judgment that I know I deserve. *That's the guy who got pulled over because he was still drunk from the night before. What an idiot.*

I inwardly cringe and focus my attention on the back of the cop's head as he leads me to the front. He stops me at a counter and has me sign a few things, then hands me back my phone, wallet and keys, rambling something about getting information about my court hearing in the mail, and handing me a pamphlet about dealing with my impounded car.

And then I'm through the doors to the front, and faced with looking at the familiar face that has been haunting me, that I just saw this morning. The one that I want to see every day except for today.

Charlie.

We stand there and stare at each other for a second before she turns on squeaky shoes and starts walking down the hallway towards the exit.

I catch up to her as she pushes through the front door and follow her outside.

"I'm sorry for calling you, but I'm not ready to tell Rachel."

"And you didn't have any other friends you could call?" she bites out, still walking at a quick pace through the parking lot.

I shrug, but realize she can't see me where I'm walking just behind her. "I just… I thought about who I would want to pick me up and it was your name that came to mind."

She stops abruptly and I nearly crash into her, but narrowly avoid a collision by lunging to the side.

"Why would you want *me* to pick you up?"

I stand there and stare at her, unsure of what to say.

Finally, I settle with, "I don't know."

She shakes her head, then turns and continues walking. I have no choice but to follow her.

"Well, I *don't* appreciate you calling me. I was at *work*, Jeremy. I had to find someone to cover my shift, and then take the bus home, and then dig around to find RJ's keys and then come drive into downtown LA traffic to get you. You should be thankful RJ left her car here when she and Mack went to the beach. Did you forget the part where I don't have a car?"

Shit. I clearly didn't think about what it would do to her day to have to come get me.

"I'm sorry, Char, really. I didn't think about that. I just…" I let my words trail off because, what am I supposed to say to her?

Did I think about anyone but myself when I called her? No. I thought about what would be easiest on me, not her. And can I tell her that even though I'd rather her pick me up than my sister, I hate that she's seeing me this way? But at the same time, how seeing her beautiful smile was the only positive thing I could focus on while sitting in the drunk tank? No, of course not. She'd laugh in my face and call me a prick. I don't deserve her kindness, so the self-deprecating part of me is somewhat thankful I'm not getting it.

When we finally reach RJ's VW bug – a cute little thing I helped her restore so she could have her own wheels during her freshman year of college – Charlie unlocks the door, climbs in, then reaches across to unlock the door on my side. Once I've settled in and we've pulled out of the parking lot, Charlie asks me the obvious question.

"What the *hell* were you thinking, Jeremy? A DUI? After everything you two have already been through with your dad? Seriously?" Her tone of voice communicates just what an idiot she thinks I am.

"I wasn't shitfaced, okay? I just still had some in me from last night." I sigh and rest my head against the back of the seat. "Did you know that most people get arrested for drunk driving in the morning on their way to work or on their way home from somewhere, when they think they've slept it off?" That bit of info had shocked me when I'd had to endure the long stream of information from the cop who drove me to the station.

But hey, the more you know.

"I don't give a shit about that, Jeremy!" she shouts at me, filling the car with her anger. "You think any person who has gotten into an accident because the other driver was drunk cares *at all* how long ago the driver had stopped drinking? Or where they were going? No! They don't." She slams her hand into the steering wheel. "What if you had hit someone?" And then her voice warbles. "Or *worse*, what if something had happened to you?"

I finally glance over at her, and I'm stunned to see tears rolling down her cheeks.

"I'm sorry," I whisper. "That's really all I can say, even though I know it's not enough."

Unbidden, my hand reaches over and wipes a tear away from her cheek. She flinches, but then just as quickly, she leans just slightly into my hand.

After a few seconds, I pull back, settling into my seat and staring out the passenger side window. We drive in silence for a while, the downtown LA traffic not having let up even though rush hour should be over.

"What is going on with you, Jeremy?"

Charlie's whispered question thrusts a knife into the comfortable silence. When I don't answer, she continues on. "I know we aren't … close. But something is different with you. RJ's noticed. Even Mack and I have noticed, and we don't normally spend any time with you. It's like…" she pauses and shrugs. "It's like the light inside you is gone."

I continue staring out the window, not really sure what to say. I've never considered myself to be a person who has a *light* inside them.

"Whatever light you think you saw… I'm not sure it was ever there to begin with," I finally say as we pull up in front of my building.

When I look at her, she's shaking her head. "You're wrong, Jeremy. You're *so* wrong." She lets out a humorless laugh. "Don't get me wrong, I don't think I really know you today. But the man I met freshman year? That man? He was a *good man*. A man with promise and life and the world at his fingertips."

She adjusts in her seat to look right at me.

"I don't know you now, but I know the goodness inside of you. I know it's still there. And yeah, maybe you're a different person now because people change. But the way you love your sister? The way you care about and support your friends? How hard you work at a craft you're so good at? Those are a light inside of you Jeremy. And for some reason, you've let that light die. RJ told me how hard you took it when she shared with you what it was like growing up in your dad's house. And I can't help but see a connection between how you're acting now and the fact that you just found out about all of that a few months ago."

She shakes her head.

"Everything seemed to take a nosedive after RJ's accident. You've been skipping out on things with her, making excuses. Don't think she hasn't talked to me about it. We're best friends. She wants you in her life. She loves you so much. And you've been pushing her away. And I think it's because you think the shit hand she was dealt was your fault."

She lets out a breath.

"Don't push away the people that love you. Don't let go of the things that are important to you. Because if you do, you're walking down a road that's been travelled before. And look how well that turned out for your dad."

My head jerks up at her statement. I don't really have a response. What do you say to all of that?

I stare blankly out the window for a minute, deciding how to respond.

"I appreciate it, Char. I do. I just..." I exhale and rub my face with my hands. "... I just don't know how to deal with how I feel about anything."

"Do you actually *know* how you feel?"

"Lost."

The word is out before I can censor it. But I know it's true. That's exactly how I feel. Lost. And alone.

"Well, if you're lost, ask the people who love you to help light your path so you can find your way again," she says, and I can't help that my lips tilt up slightly at how cheesy she sounds. But at the same time, I know how genuine she's being right now.

"I know it sounds cheesy," she adds, "but family and friends are in our lives to be our guideposts. They help us figure things out when we feel like we can't handle it on our own."

I feel this welling in my chest at her words. I've only cried one other time in my life, and this is how it felt. When Rachel told me our dad had abused her after I moved away to college, I felt like I was dying inside. But back then, I was crying because of what happened to someone else.

This time, I feel like there's a ball in my chest that just wants to be broken open. It's begging for it, as if by shattering it, somehow I can make it better.

It's like the time I broke my nose in junior high and the doctor said I'd waited too long to get it fixed.

"We have to re-break it so we can set it properly," he'd said.

I was so confused. How would breaking something fix it? It didn't make any sense.

"If you let something broken sit for too long, it starts to heal on it's own, but in the wrong way. It can cause a lot of pain and problems down the road. So even though the discomfort is painful now, in the long run, you're setting yourself up to heal properly."

Those words from almost fifteen years ago wrap themselves around the ball in my chest and squeeze until I can't take it anymore.

"I have to go," I say, abruptly.

The sweet and caring smile on Charlie's face drops slightly, sympathy appearing in its place.

"Call me if you need anything, okay?" she asks.

I just nod, open the door and climb out of the car. Before shutting the door, I lean down and look at her. "Charlie," I say. When she looks back at me, the feelings

I've felt for her for four years bubble over. "I never should have let you go."

The startled look on her face is enough to let me know I've said too much. But even though I just may have, I can't bring myself to add those words to my growing list of regrets.

CHAPTER ELEVEN
Jeremy

March

"So what did the judge say?"

My coach is leaning against his desk, his arms crossed and eyes glaring at me. It wasn't my preferred choice to share with him that I'd been arrested for a DUI, but anytime you play professional sports, there's an image component that can't be ignored, even in a sport that gets minimal attention in the US, like soccer. So I had to let both Coach Kilzer and my agent, Bonnie, know about what happened.

Bonnie went into full damage control mode, talking to me about what I could and could not say, and what responses to use if I was asked by anyone about the 'unfortunate incident,' as she refers to it.

Coach has had a slightly different reaction. He's furious, I'm sure. But also a bit sad. I think he'd pegged me as one of the ones who wouldn't cause him any problems. So not only does he have to deal with the fact that this *is* a problem, he also has to accept the fact that he might have been wrong about me.

Hopefully, I'm able to convince him that this was a one-time mistake and not something he has to be concerned about in the long run.

"Five thousand bucks, one year probation, six month license suspension, and mandatory community service," I reply.

I let my eyes flick around his office. It's not somewhere I have to be very often, mostly because he reserves this space for things that are a bit more sensitive. Comfortable couches and muted colors, with splashes of the Galaxy blue and gold. Only a few personal things are scattered around, mostly artwork on his cabinets from his daughter.

He nods in response to the outcome of my sentencing hearing earlier this week, and rubs a finger back and forth across his chin in thought.

"Well," he finally says, "the fines and license suspension and probation are your own problem, so make sure you get that shit sorted. But I might have a connection for you on the community service thing."

"Yeah, okay." I lean forward in my chair and rest my elbows on my knees. "What do you have in mind?"

He stands from where he's been leaning against his desk and walks around it, taking a seat in his desk chair and clicking onto his computer.

"I have a buddy that runs a youth sports league in Burbank for at-risk kids. I'm pretty sure he sent me an email about finding some players to volunteer with the basketball team." He clicks a few more times, then glances at me. "You played basketball in high school, right?" At my nod, he flicks his eyes back to his screen. "I'll take a look at it and see what can happen. I don't know for sure if it will count as community service, but once I have the details, I'll get them to you so you can check with your lawyer."

Relief rushes through me. A community service project like working with at-risk kids is much less risky from a PR standpoint than cleaning up litter on the side of the highway.

"That would be great. Thanks, Coach."

He's silent for just long enough that I think that's my cue to leave, so I stand and make my way over to the door.

"You know, Jameson, I never thought you'd be one of the ones that would get into a mess like this," I hear from behind me just as I put my hand on the doorknob.

My head drops.

So close.

I turn to look at him. "Well, I hope to show you it was just one misstep and you won't have to worry about it happening again."

He nods from where he's seated at his desk, leaning back in his chair and hands interlocked on his stomach. "Yeah, I figured you'd say something like that. And I believe you mean it, too."

He stands and walks towards me.

"You know, my best friend when I played league ball eons ago was a lot like you."

I groan internally, knowing this monologue isn't leading anywhere good.

"He was incredibly smart, charismatic and great on the field."

My chest puffs a bit at the compliment, something that doesn't come often from Coach.

"He was a marketing dream, and we were all a bit jealous, if I'm completely honest. But you can't help it when someone just has that *it* factor, you know? He was able to wow everyone in pretty much every aspect of his life." He pauses. "We didn't notice the drinking problem at first."

My stomach launches itself into my throat, and my eyes drop to the floor.

"You chalk it up to living the dream life, you know? He's just an athlete enjoying his time in the limelight. But I knew something was wrong when I'd find him drinking alone, in the quiet of his sprawling house."

I close my eyes. "Coach…"

"It was a deeper problem. There was something eating at him and he used alcohol to numb it. It ended up ruining his career and shattered the relationships he had with his family and friends. We offered him help and support, tried to get him involved in AA. Nothing took. And then the drinking spiraled to drug use."

"Coach, I swear to you…"

"Jeremy, I'm not trying to tell you I think you're suicidal or need to be watched like a hawk, okay?" He lets out an exhausted breath. "I just want to make sure you have someone tell you *now*, while it's still early on, that you can find healthier alternatives to dealing with whatever is eating you alive."

I don't know what to say. So I don't say anything and just fixate my eyes on the wall behind him, my hands resting on my hips.

"We care about you here, Jeremy. I know things with your sister and dad have been rough for a while." My eyes shoot to his. "Your agent called to let me know in case you missed any practices. Which would have been understandable. But you didn't miss a single one. Some people would call that dedication. And at some point in my career, I might have agreed with them. But I know what's important in life now, much more than I did when I was in the sunrise of my pro career."

I see his eyes briefly lock onto the lone photo of his daughter that sits on his small conference table.

"It doesn't make you less dedicated or weak to take time to focus on something that is more important than soccer," he says. "The truth is – and if you repeat this to anyone, I'll deny every word – there should be a lot in your life that is more important than what happens on that field."

That ball in my chest is growing, the pressure enough to make me feel slightly sick. I've been an emotional mess over the past six weeks, ever since Charlie picked me up from the station and tried to get me to open up.

I clear my throat. Then clear it again.

"Thanks, Coach. I really do appreciate it. And I know it sounds like I'm bullshitting you, but I really do have things under control."

He plops a hand on my shoulder and gives me a sad smile, then takes a step back and turns towards his desk.

"I'll have more info for you later today about the sports league. Make sure to check your email."

I say my thanks one more time, then hightail it out of the office before he can add anything else.

As horrible as this may sound, there are some perks to having to hire a driver to get around. I should have considered this a long time ago, but always thought it was a bit too self-indulgent. I mean, I'm not David Beckham.

Malory is sitting inside of the already air conditioned SUV when I walk out front. Once I've gotten settled in the back, he begins the forty-five minute, traffic-congested drive to my house. I take the time to flick through my phone and answer a few emails. I've lived in SoCal my entire life and I have to say, having a driver handle this traffic while I mess around on my phone is definitely not the worst.

Once we pull into my spot in the underground lot beneath my building, he stays with the car, and I head upstairs. Part of me feels like a prick for essentially hiring someone to sit around and wait for me. But, what am I gonna do? Take the bus?

I chuckle to myself at the thought.

Once I make it inside, I change into my workout gear and hit the building gym for a much-needed chance to get rid of some excess energy. When I get back to my apartment an hour later, tired in the best way, I find a new email alert.

To: Jeremy Jameson
From: Robert Kilzer
Subject: Community Service

Jameson,

Patrick Gary is the guy organizing the at-risk youth sports league in Burbank. He's thrilled to have

*you help. He asked if you know anyone who can be
your second. I figure you could ask one of the guys,
but you might have a friend or something you'd
rather ask?*

*Regardless, make sure to contact him in the next
day or so. He can give you more info that you can
share with your lawyer to make sure it all clears the
community service requirements.*

*And think about what I said. Let me know if I
can do anything for you.*

Coach

At the bottom is Patrick's contact info. I immediately
give him a call as I grab a water bottle from the fridge.

"Patrick Gary."

"Hi Patrick, my name is Jeremy Jameson. Coach
Kilzer said I should reach out to you about helping with
the youth league?" I take a swig of my water and post up
at the bar in my kitchen.

"Oh, hey man!" he says, his tone of voice completely
changing. "Yeah, thanks for giving me a call. I'm in a real
bind, here, and would really appreciate some extra hands."

"Well I would love to help. So how do I get started?"

"I'll send you the details so you can forward them to
your lawyer," he says, and I cringe. I mean, we both know
why I need to find a way to do community service, but I
hate hearing it said out loud. "I'll also include the practice
schedule and curriculum. We do a two-hour weekly practice on Thursday evenings. You start with some physical

activity, and tie in some evidence-based curriculum to help share with students why getting involved in athletics can help them long-term. It's only about twenty minutes of each practice, so don't worry that I'll have you reading from a textbook," he says with a laugh.

"And then you take them into a normal practice. Hey, you wouldn't happen to know anyone who can help, would you? It's really a program built to be done in pairs. The other person doesn't even have to know anything about sports, they just have to be able to act as your assistant. Pass things out, keep track of players, handle the waivers and some of the gear."

"I'm... well, I haven't really shared with anyone that I have to do community service, so, I don't think there's really anyone..."

But I let my voice trail off.

Maybe there is someone.

Someone who doesn't know anything about sports but would be great at keeping things organized.

"Actually, I might have someone."

"Absolutely not."

"Come on Charlie. I've never asked you to do me a favor before."

"Jeremy, you have got to be joking. First of all, you asked me to pick you up from the police station after your DUI. If I were to categorize that request it would be in the favors category. Second, not only do I know nothing about basketball, I'm incredibly busy with my final semester of college. You remember college? It's that thing you have to do in order to be a contributing member of society."

I roll my eyes, thankful she can't see me through the phone. She is equal parts adorable and exasperating.

"I went to college, Char, I remember."

"So then, you'll understand why I'm saying no."

"Charlie. Please. I'm not ready to share with anyone else what happened, and you're really the only person apart from my Coach and lawyer and agent who know about it."

"So ask one of *them*."

I laugh. "You're crazy, you know that right?"

I know she's cranky at me, but I can hear her smile over the phone when she says, "I've always known that."

I let out a sigh.

"Look, Charlie. I wouldn't be asking you if I had another option, okay?" Technically, it's true. "It's once a week, and if you can't get things sorted out with work, you can just skip those practices or something. It's only a twelve-week program, so if you have to miss a few, it's not a big deal."

There's silence on the other end.

"Aren't you the one who just told me I need to start reaching out more and not pushing people away?"

She groans.

"Yeah, well, I meant mostly RJ when I said that. But I'll sound like a hypocrite if I say no when you're finally clawing your way out of whatever funk you've been in."

"I'm not clawing my way out of anyth…"

"I'll do it, Jeremy," she says, interrupting me and putting a smile on my face. "Just… send me the details or whatever."

"*Thank you,* Charlie. You have no idea how much I appreciate this."

"Yeah, well…" and she trails off.

"Check your email tonight, okay?"

"Sounds good."

"And Charlie?"

"Yeah?"

"Let me know if you need any tutoring on what a basketball *court* is, okay?"

She huffs and then the call ends.

Maybe that wasn't the smartest way to wrap things up, but it sure was funny.

CHAPTER TWELVE
Jeremy

March

"It wasn't *that* bad."

I glance over to where Charlie sits, fuming, in the seat next to mine. Malory is at the wheel and navigating us through traffic after our first practice with the kiddos, and to say Charlie was bit out of her element is an understatement.

"Fuck off, Jeremy," she bites at me, her face practically glued to the window as she stares out at the city passing us by.

When I bark out a laugh, she turns and glares.

"Oh, come on," I say, trying to get her to loosen up a bit. "So, you could maybe brush up on your terminology or something. But those kids? They're *looking* for a reason to be pissed off at someone. You just happened to be their target today."

"Well, I don't know if acting as target practice is a good idea for me." And then she's back to facing the window.

I take her in where she sits next to me, her chestnut hair tied back in one French braid that drops down to just past her shoulders. She normally wears her hair down, except when she's in her adorable scrubs, but I love when she pulls it back off of her neck. So sexy.

I clear my throat and shift in my seat.

This is the time to be convincing her to keep helping me, not getting turned on from looking at her *neck*.

"Charlie, I'd be happy to tutor you on basketball so you don't feel so lost next week."

Her stiff posture relaxes slightly and she turns towards me.

"No, thanks. I'll just – figure it out myself. I mean, I might not be in to sports, but I'm smart. How hard can it be to do a quick refresher?"

I laugh again. "Is that what we're gonna call it? I'm pretty sure it's only a *refresher* if you need a *refresh* on things you already understand. You need a Basketball 101 class."

She lets out a tiny laugh and lets out a sigh.

"It'll be better next week, okay?"

She nods then sits back in her seat, finally getting comfortable.

"Hey, where are we going?" she asks.

"I'm gonna take you to dinner to say thank you for helping," I reply, my eyes peeking at her, trying to maintain the picture of nonchalance.

"Were you going to *tell* me you were taking me to dinner at any point?"

I shrug. "Would you have said yes if I had?"

Her silence answers my question.

A few minutes pass.

"So, what are we eating?"

I smile. "Burgers."

Fifteen minutes later, we're seated in a red and white booth at the In-N-Out Burger near Charlie and Rachel's apartment, noshing on the best burgers in the world. And Charlie doesn't disappoint. I've seen her eat a handful of times, and she always puts away enough to feed a linebacker. Where does she put it?

"You're staring."

"Yeah, well, you're easy to stare at," I reply, chomping into my Double-Double.

She rolls her eyes.

"I don't know why you're making that face, pretty girl. You know I think you're gorgeous."

She smiles a little but it doesn't quite meet her eyes

"So tell me," she says, pushing her fries and burger off to the side only three-quarters eaten. I know it must be serious if she's pushing her food away to say something. "Why did you ask me to be a part of this little basketball thing when I know nothing about sports. And be honest. I hate this bullshit about asking me because I am the only person who knows about the DUI. I think that's ridiculous and you're a fool if you think I'll believe it."

I swallow, the bite of burger I just took falling fast and hard like a rock into the pit of my stomach.

Well go ahead and just call me out on it, then.

I wipe my mouth and let out a small, embarrassed chuckle.

"That obvious, huh?"

She nods.

"Okay, well…" I scratch the back of my head and then lean forward, resting my elbows on the table. "If I am completely, one hundred percent honest, no filter… it's because I wanted to spend time with you. I always want to spend time with you. I've always *wanted* to spend time with you. And this felt like a good enough excuse."

She watches me, and I can tell by her expression that she's unconvinced.

"What do you want me to say, Charlie? That I regret how things started and stopped with us so quickly? You have to know it's because I didn't want to hurt Rachel. She told me you two have talked about it – quite a few times, in fact. It shouldn't be a shock that she told me you were off limits back then. She didn't want my dick to potentially ruin things. She just didn't know when she told me that we had already gone out."

She looks down at her hands, where she's tearing a napkin apart on the table.

"You can't expect me to believe that if RJ hadn't said anything to you that we would have gone on more dates, Jeremy. I knew what I was getting myself into with you, and I got exactly what I originally thought I would get. The only reason I was hurt at the end was because you'd said things that had me believing we would be going on more dates and spending more time together. But I knew enough about you to know that wasn't ever going to be true."

She trails off and I clench my hands in fists, frustrated that I've never been able to tell her what that period of time was like, that I was more interested in her than I'd ever been in anyone. That I still am.

"Is it that shocking to you that I would want more from you?"

She stares at me blankly, not letting anything away.

"Charlie, I *did* want to continue things. There's no reason for me to blow smoke up your ass about that, okay? I *did*. And I *always* regretted that I didn't just tell Rachel that I was interested in you. It's not like she would have never spoken to me again. I'm her brother and her favorite person ever."

She rolls her eyes.

"But if I'm honest? Again, brutally honest?" I say, knowing I might be shooting myself in the foot. "I don't know if it would have been a good idea. Back then… well, back then, maybe I wasn't ready. For you, I mean. You're this amazing, thoughtful person who always puts other people first, and I was this selfish guy who just wanted to get laid all the time."

She lets out a humorless chuckle.

"And I'm not talking about you when I say that. Yes, that night was amazing. Am I going to tell you it was the best sex I've ever had in my entire life? No. I'm not. Because that would be a lie, and I'm done lying about anything with you."

Her mouth drops open and she looks equal parts shocked and offended.

"But I'm not telling you that because it was bad. It was amazing. It was absolutely *fucking* amazing. And I can tell you right now, it was absolutely the most meaningful night I've ever had. I've never felt like that before, and I haven't come even close to feeling like that since. I can't tell you why. I can't tell you what was so amazing about that night except for the fact it was with you."

I take a breath and pause, because Charlie looks so startled.

And upset.

Wait, I didn't mean to upset her. I just wanted to be honest.

"So like I said, I regret calling things off, but I wonder if it was for the best. It gave me a chance to grow up a little bit. See what it was like without you, and really narrow things down so I *knew* what I was doing. Because back then? I didn't have a clue. I just knew I had to keep away from you. So I did. But I don't feel like that anymore, Charlie."

I reach over and take her hands.

"I've never stopped wanting you."

She stares where my hands are over hers, her eyes glassy. She doesn't say anything for so long, I worry what's going through her mind.

"So, I'm supposed to jump at the chance to be with you now that you've gotten everything out of your system?"

I'm startled by her words and I squeeze her hands as she tries to pull them away.

"Charlie… that's *not* what I'm trying to say, here. At all."

But she's shaking her head, and I know that whatever part of her wants to believe me is being strangled by the part of her that thinks I'm an ass. That *knows* I'm an ass.

"You have no idea what everything you just said is doing to me right now," she says. "I think you think your words are going to have this swoon effect where I just crumble because *hooray you finally decided it was time to put your dick away and go after something meaningful.* But what about how that makes me feel, huh? To know that you've spent *years* caring about me and wanting me and doing nothing about it? I couldn't have been *that* important. Definitely not to the level that you think we should magically be together like nothing ever happened."

She wipes a hand at a lone tear streaking her cheek.

"And I hate to break it to you, Jeremy, but I don't want to have a relationship that's on the whim of your *feelings,* because – no offense – it seems like those are as consistent and reliable as the weatherman. Your feelings blow you all over the place, and I don't want to be involved in that storm. I have enough bullshit going on in my own life and don't need to worry constantly whether you're feeling in love with me today or not. Love isn't a feeling – it's a *verb.* It's an action word, Jeremy. It's something you do, not how you feel. And you have literally done nothing to show me that you have anything for me other than feelings that will sway wherever the wind blows you."

She chuckles humorlessly again, the self-deprecation in her voice clear.

"And you want me to believe you've *grown up*, or *changed* so much since you were a senior in college? How's that?"

She lifts a finger to start counting.

"There's the fact that I've seen you hooking up with girls at least three times since the fall, all different people. And that's *just* the times when I was *at* the parties or bars where you were."

She lifts a second finger and I feel my cheeks heat.

"There's the fact that you've been nursing your problems with alcohol and got arrested."

She lifts another one.

"There's the whole drama with RJ and her boyfriend, who you manipulated by threatening his job."

She finally puts her hands down, and her face relaxes slightly.

"I'm not trying to be a bitch, Jeremy. I'm just pointing out very obvious things that point to a strong possibility that you still have quite a bit of growing up to do."

It's clear she's finished now, because she picks up her burger and practically shoves the entire thing in her face.

I'd want to laugh if I didn't feel so gutted.

What was I thinking by sharing all of that shit with her? That she'd realize I was worthy of her? That she'd fall into my arms, like she said I was hoping for?

I'd never even thought about how she might react, so sure things would work out the way I envisioned. It's exactly what did when I had her pick me up from the police station. And then what I did again when I pushed her into helping me with the basketball team.

God, how fucking self-absorbed have I been?

"Charlie..." I start, but I'm not sure what to say.

"Look, Jeremy," she pauses and wipes her face with a napkin. "What I said in the car? About you needing to look to the people who love you for help? I really did mean that. And even though things have always been weird between us, you've been this peripheral part of my life since I met RJ. You're important, and I don't know if that will ever change. I *do* want to be helpful, in whatever way I can."

She grabs her bag and sets it in her lap, looping her hands through the strap like it is the only shield she has from me.

Gotta be honest. It feels like shit to see that.

"I will always be here for you. But as a friend. I just can't see us being anything more than that, okay? It's not because I don't care for you. I just feel like we have very different ideas of what relationships should look like."

She lets out a sigh and stretches out her neck.

"I spent... god, *years* doing things the wrong way. But over the summer, I realized that if I wanted something more than the shitty guys I was screwing around with, I had to stop screwing around with shitty guys."

She shrugs.

"But I didn't get there overnight, you know? First, it took a few months of going out and *not* going home with someone. It took reminding myself that what I actually wanted would take time to nurture, and grow, and isn't likely to happen because someone bought me some drinks and we fucked in his car."

I swallow down the bitterness I get at that picture.

"I started focusing more on the things that matter to me. I started doing the things that *I* love, and focusing more on school and my career. And you know what? I've only been on two dates since getting back from summer. But they were *good dates,* even though they didn't end in getting into a relationship. And you know why? Because I *learned* something from them. I've never slept with a guy and then felt like I learned something other than what I do or don't like in bed. But everything we do in life should teach us something, and I decided I wanted to have relationships that challenge me to grow and be a better person. And Jeremy, as wonderful as you are, you're just not there."

I rub my face, scratch my head, anything to give me a reprieve from looking at those eyes of her that look so betrayed. She's still so hurt by how I treated her. How I've continued to treat her.

"I can't help that I've been focused on this over the past eight months and you've been doing the same old thing. How am I supposed to believe that you've been pining for me when you're still screwing people and..."

"I'm not."

She pauses.

"It's been almost six months, Charlie. I haven't been able to think about anyone but you."

She leans back in her chair, taking my words in. Digesting them.

"And I know you're gonna think I'm full of shit – and who knows, maybe I am – but this thing I feel for you? It's not going away. It's just not." I rub the back of my neck to ease the tension I feel. "And I realize that I have to prove that to you, and that it's gonna take time. And I'm okay with that."

She's shaking her head.

"No, Charlie, don't shake your head. Don't shut this down. I know right now, you think I'm blowing smoke. But that just means I need to show you I'm serious. I might have fucked up. I might not have made all of the right choices. I might have actively made some bad ones over the past few months. But that's not who I want to be. It's not who *you* make me want to be."

I lean forward again.

"I want to be a better man for you. I want to be the person you believe I can be."

She's giving me this look I can't decipher, somewhere

between hope and sadness.

"But you can't be that person for *me*, Jeremy. You have to make that change for *you.*" She sighs. "Don't you see that? Don't you realize that if you make changes for me, and then we start something and fall apart, you wont know who you are anymore? You have to want to change because *you* want to."

"I do. Fuck." I fist a hand in my hair. "I'm not explaining myself very well."

I suck down a sip of my soda and she sits in silence.

"Charlie just... promise me something okay?"

She just stares at me.

"Promise me that you won't permanently close the door on anything happening between us okay? I'm not saying you have to promise me a date. I'm not saying you have to promise anything other than your potential consideration in the future."

She sighs again.

A minute ticks by.

And just when I think she isn't going to respond, she does.

"Okay."

CHAPTER THIRTEEN
Charlie

April

"Hey Coach D?"

I turn at the sound of my name, poised with a clipboard and pen. I know I look ridiculous in my striped referee shirt and a whistle wrapped around my neck, but I can't help that these kids made me want to learn about basketball.

That's right... the *kids* made me want to learn about basketball. It wasn't Jeremy.

Definitely not.

"Yes, Jaime. What can I do for you?"

While Jaime launches into a detailed backstory before asking his question, I let my eyes drift over across the court to where Jeremy is working with a group of kids on free throws.

God, he looks delicious in those little shorts. I don't know where guys got the idea that women appreciate really baggy clothing, because I can guarantee it isn't true.

Who wants to see some guy with a droopy ass? No. Keep those shorts short, baby.

Jeremy doesn't subscribe to the mentality that the typical male college students do. His outfit fits him *just right*. His basketball shorts look fit but comfortable, are an appropriate length, not showing off ten inches of underwear or hanging down to his ankles. His LA Galaxy tank is also just loose enough to give his body some breathing room without being grotesque in how much muscle is showing. But you better believe it does that too. And I can't keep my eyes off him, even though I *should* be focusing on keeping the kids moving through their drills rotation.

It's been about a month since his little declaration over burgers, and I've had to work very hard not to let myself get bowled over by him.

Because, *damn*, the man is doing everything in his power to win me over. And what's worse? I don't think he even realizes that what he's doing is starting to win me over.

Because he isn't doing anything blatant. He isn't asking me on dates. He isn't declaring his love for me. He isn't trying to prove to me that he's changed his playboy ways.

He's just... changing.

I haven't seen him parked outside of our house asleep. He shows up to every practice with that positive energy that was missing after everything that happened with RJ. He takes me for dinner after every practice and we just talk, our conversations staying light and fun. And on the one night I had to miss practice because I couldn't swap shifts, he drove over to my hospital and dropped off dinner for me. The little note inside the bag said *Because we couldn't have dinner together tonight, I'm dropping off a sandwich for you. I'm eating one too – feel free to give me a call if you want to chat on your break.*

My break that night was at 2am, so I'd shot him a text to let him know. Much to my surprise, I got a call from him at 2:01. His sleepy voice was so sexy over the phone and yanked me back down memory lane, to the one and only morning I woke up in his bed.

"Does that sound okay?"

Jaime's question snaps me back to the present and I glance down at him. I say *down* like the twelve-year-old isn't barely an inch shorter than me, which is ridiculous. I'm fucking tall.

"I'm sorry, what?"

"Can my brother Andre join the team?"

"Isn't your brother, like, in the third grade?"

He shrugs.

"Jaime, there are definitely chances for him to get involved. There's a team for his age group. If you want, I can make sure the guy in charge gives your parents a call?"

He shakes his head. "But the kids his age pick on him. I want him to be here so he can know he's safe, you know?"

I wrap my arm around Jaime and give him a squeeze, so touched at his desire to protect his younger brother. "Sweetie, I know that must be hard on you. And it would be really easy to blow it under the rug and say they're just teasing and it's just what happens in elementary school. But sometimes getting picked on makes going to school and stuff the *worst.*"

Jaime nods.

"But think about myself and Coach J, okay? Do you

think we would stand for that if someone was getting picked on at practice here?"

He shakes his head.

"Exactly. And there's a team of two in charge of the team that will be the right age group for Andre. Wanna know what else? There are kids from all of the school districts on this team. You and Cruz have been getting along great, right?

He nods again in reference to a kid that Jaime seems to play around with alot.

"And doesn't Cruz go to a different school than you? Wouldn't it be so awesome for Andre to join a team and then make new friends his own age? People that also want to play basketball and have fun together?"

"I guess," he says on a shrug, not looking entirely convinced.

I laugh and press a hand to my chest. "Don't sound so excited. You're gonna bowl me over with your enthusiasm, mister!"

He smiles.

"There's the smile I was looking for. Okay, now I'll have Patrick call your parents this week to see if we can get Andre on the team for his age, alright? Just keep things positive and encouraging for him."

"Thanks, Coach D."

And with that, Jaime runs off and joins up with Jeremy again.

I never thought I would actually enjoy the practices. I hate athleticism in general when it comes to my own self. My body just doesn't work that way. I have pretty much zero muscles on this frame of mine. The whole jogging-as-a-new-years-resolution thing petered out about a week after it started, turning into more of a morning stroll once or twice a week, if I'm not too tired.

But the practices have actually, surprisingly, been fantastic. Once I started studying up on basketball, I didn't feel so lost. Not only did it make the kids take me a little more seriously, but it also seriously helped when I made my March Madness bracket with my friends. To say Jeremy was surprised by the fact that I picked so many of the correct teams is an understatement. He said it was beginners luck. I say it's because my brain is fucking amazing.

"Alright everyone, let's huddle up!"

Jeremy's whistle calls the end of practice and everyone jogs over to center court. As we circle around him, he crouches low and starts talking about what went well in practice, taking time to add in the light material assigned by his boss to touch on topics relevant to the at-risk component of this league.

And as he stands there, reiterating what he said last week about teamwork and family, I wonder if maybe I wrote him off too quickly when he said he wanted me to give him another chance. I mean, people can change, right?

"Okay, so our first game is this weekend," he says. "Just a reminder to be here at 10am on Saturday morning. I'll have your jerseys and some snacks too. And make sure to get some rest tomorrow. No barhopping the night before a game, okay?"

The kids all laugh at that, and Jeremy flashes his trademark grin at their amusement.

"Alright, Lions on three!"

"How was practice?"

I drop my bag and kick off my shoes at the door, then wander into the living room, where I find RJ sprawled out on the couch with the TV on and a book and notebook on her lap.

"Pretty good today, actually. I think I kind of bonded with one of the kids. Which is great. It makes me feel good to know that they're getting another adult in their lives that reminds them they matter."

She smiles, picking up her phone. "Awesome. I was about to order some Chinese food. You want in?"

I shake my head, sinking into the couch next to her. "Jeremy took me to get tacos on the way home from practice."

She nods, slowly, and I can tell there's something she wants to say. It's like her words are sitting on the tip of her tongue and she can't seem to just spit them out at me.

"Whatever you want to say, just say it."

"It just seems," she says immediately, like she was waiting for me to give her the green light, "like you and Jeremy are spending an awful lot of time together. Is all. You know. That I wanted to say. That's it."

I laugh.

"Jeremy and I are trying to be friends, now. I already told you this."

She rolls her eyes. "Well that's stupid. You both acknowledge that me telling Jeremy not to date you is why he broke things off freshman year. And I've told you – repeatedly over the past few months it seems like – that I overreacted freshman year because I was just so protective of our new friendship. Now that we've all gotten over the bygones from yesteryear, you should just start dating.

Like, I don't get the problem."

I sigh.

"RJ, we didn't not date because of you. There were…
a bunch of reasons things wouldn't have worked out back
then. Not just the fact that you share the same DNA."

I stick my feet out on the coffee table and sink further
into the couch, hoping she'll let it go.

"But come on!" she says, raising her arms above her
head like a child who doesn't understand why they cant
have their Christmas present *right now*, just because she
wants it, even though it's April. "You guys would be so
cute together."

I laugh. "Well… while that may be true, I think your
brother is going through something and needs to focus on
himself. And I have…" I gesture out at nothing, "… my
own stuff going on."

"Oh really? Your own stuff?"

I nod, tucking myself into the corner of the couch
and resting my head against the arm.

"Wasn't it not so long ago that a certain someone was
pushing *me* to step outside of my comfort zone and pur-
sue a relationship? Hmmmm?"

I smile at her. RJ has turned into a hopeless romantic
ever since things got sorted out with her man. They do
adorable things like cook together and set the kitchen
table to have living room dates. And now I'm seeing that
lightheartedness that can only come from feeling content
pouring from her.

"RJ, I love you, and I will happily let you wax poetic
about something romantic happening between myself and
your oh-so-sexy brother," – she makes a slight gagging
noise – "but we just aren't there, okay? I have to focus on

the last few weeks of college, as do *you.*" She narrows her eyes and huffs. "And Jeremy? He has to, like, learn to be an adult or something."

RJ laughs, a fully belly laugh much larger than she is erupting out of her tiny frame.

"Learn to be an adult? Are you kidding me?" She laughs again. "Jeremy is *always* the adult, even when he's being a stupidface."

I wince inwardly. RJ still doesn't know about Jeremy's DUI. She doesn't know that he's battling with himself about his responsibility to her, about the fault that he believes lies with him over the abuse she experienced growing up.

He's keeping it all bottled up, which any good self-help book will tell you is the worst way to deal with something. It's like he thinks if he shares how he's struggling with RJ, something bad will happen. Maybe he just doesn't want to burden her with anything else after everything she dealt with. I don't know, but I want to try and help him work through it.

It's a dangerous little thing we are doing, and subconsciously – maybe even consciously – I know that my involvement with him now, while I say it's platonic, is anything but.

CHAPTER FOURTEEN
Charlie

April

Graduation is three weeks away.

I look at the four tickets I'm holding in my hand, the embossed lettering and swirly bullshit announcing the culmination of a four-year adventure. Every graduate gets four tickets.

No more, no less.

I heard once that some of the students who don't need all four tickets auction them off at some underground night during grad week, some of them going for as high as five hundred bucks. When I mentioned it to RJ, her eyes lit up like it was the most amazing thing she'd ever heard.

I'm pretty sure she's inviting her brother, her boyfriend and her boss from the part-time job she's had since freshman year, which would leave her one extra ticket to auction off.

Me, on the other hand… I'll need all four.

Maybe.

If I can convince everyone to come.

If I can convince *anyone* to come.

I dread the conversation with my parents. They aren't horrible people, by any means. But they just don't get me. They still think the whole nursing thing is a mistake. They still want me to just find a man and settle down and have kids, like my older sister. Issy has two kids now. How you can meet someone, get married and have two entire human children only three and a half years later is mind blowing to me. Didn't she have anything else she wanted to do?

I sigh and flick through the contacts on my phone.

And then I feel like an asshole because I know that getting married and starting a family is *exactly* what she wanted to do and I should be happy for her. I shouldn't be upset that she didn't do what *I* think should make her happy.

Mom and dad and Issy will come to the graduation. That's not the issue. It's that I'm going to invite my brother, who hasn't seen or talked to my parents since he graduated high school and moved to New York. I get why that happened, and support my brother. When your dad tells you that being gay is a phase and that you just need to keep the exploration to yourself, there are only so many options you have on how to deal with it. My brother wanted to be out and proud, which is hard to do when you live in a tiny town in a red state full of conservative minds.

Grey and I talk a few times a month. He's living a fun life, working as a waiter and going to school for architecture. I always tease him that he should have gone to cosmetology school and used all those nights when I did his makeup to his advantage. He just laughs and says, "Come on, Lee-Lee, quit with the stereotyping."

When I find the Davenport section of my contacts list, I hesitate, my thumb hovering over which number I want to call first. If I call my parents, I'll be on the phone forever and they'll have all sorts of questions for me about what my plans are and whether I've gotten a job yet and am I dating someone. If I call Grey, he'll get stuck on the cost of the ticket, and then we'll end up in an awkward conversation about whether mom and dad will even talk to him and whether it's worth it to fly all the way out to California for just a few days if they're gonna be ignoring him the entire time.

So I chicken out and flick off two texts. One to Grey and one to my parents and sister.

> *Me: Grey baby, graduation is May 12th. I've got your ticket in my hand! Can't wait to see you. Text me your flight details once you get it sorted.*

> *Me: Hey everyone, I finally have the graduation tickets. Can't wait to see you on the 12th! I'll email you a link to the full schedule. Love you!*

Then I put my phone down and lean my head back on the headrest, my headache making me want to call in sick for the first time since I started my clinical rotation at Glendale Adventist. I've been here since the start of junior year, and I've never missed a single day.

I glance at the side entrance and watch doctors and

nurses coming and going, starting or ending shifts. There's an eerie calm that overtakes you when you're going into an environment as chaotic as a hospital. It's almost like your body knows that you have to be calm in order to exist in such a place.

I really do enjoy working here. It has always been my dream, to help people, to find a way to make others' lives better, even if it's just with a smile and caring hands. I love those times when I get to see kids who need someone to give them a positive attitude when they're all scraped up, or when I get to make things less scary for the person that's never been in a hospital before.

But what I really enjoy is going through rooms and chatting with the people who seem to be here alone. There's a sadness that permeates hospital walls. It's like a unique form of cancer that can suck life out of people who don't have anyone by their side when they're wondering what's happening with their body. Sometimes, if I let myself focus on it for too long, I can feel it leeching the natural optimism from my body, leaving only the rumblings of melancholy behind.

During my junior year, I cried after having to help a single mother with her newborn. The mom had been so clearly alone and scared for her little guy that needed stitches. But she had also been brave, so focused on making sure her son's needs were taken care of. Of course, I was a brand new intern without really any capabilities to help her other than asking her how she was doing and trying to provide encouragement and support. By the time she left a few hours later, she had a smile on her face – an exhausted smile that didn't entirely reach her eyes, but it was better than the look of loneliness and feeling of being lost that had been stamped on her face when she first arrived.

I'd said my goodbyes and stolen away to a little closet near my station, letting the tears fall for a few minutes before returning to work. My supervisor had seen me, and decided to have a pretty firm chat with me about not getting too emotionally involved.

"There are too many sad stories, Charlotte," he'd said. "If you let yourself get upset about all of them, you'll never make it. And you have to be here, physically and mentally, if you really want to make a difference."

So now, every time I come to work, I have to put on my Nurse Charlie mask. The one in a permanently pleasant expression, with kind words but not too much empathy or sympathy. The one that helps but doesn't get attached.

But I feel like this façade is just as draining as it is to emotionally invest in my patients. I'm looking forward to wrapping up my time here and starting my full-time job after graduation.

I haven't told anyone, but I've gotten a job at Pasadena Village, the facility where Nan lives. It's basically grunt work, but I get to be there with the patients and spend some more time popping in on my hooligan of a grandmother. She's still a firecracker, that's for sure. But the past few years have taken a toll on her. And I want more than anything to make sure she knows she isn't forgotten.

Because, well, isn't that what any of us wants? To know we are loved and cared for? Not just sitting alone in an elderly home when things are nearing the end?

I sigh, shaking off the emotions that have been wrapping themselves around me over the past fifteen minutes as I've sat in RJ's car, avoiding going in any earlier than I have to.

My roommate and her boyfriend have gone out of town on some fancy getaway, leaving me with the keys to her tiny little death trap of a car. Normally I take the bus to work, which works very well for me. The aggressiveness of the average California driver is enough to send me flying out of my skin on any given day.

But when my shift ends tomorrow morning at 7am, I'll only have a little bit of time to get home, shower, change and head over to Burbank to help with the basketball game. With time super tight, I have to move as quickly as possible.

I sigh again.

I don't know what the hell I'm doing, or why Jeremy wants me involved.

No, wait. That's a lie.

I know why he wants me involved. He wants to spend time with me. Which would be great if it didn't set off an explosion of butterflies and nerves every time we're together. It's like my brain logically knows that he needs some time to sort out his life before I should even consider starting something up with him.

But how do I tell that to my poor little heart? The heart that has been secretly – okay, maybe not-so-secretly – pining for Jeremy since that first meeting in my room freshman year. How do you listen to what your mind is telling you when your heart is screaming at you that you're making a mistake?

But I'm scared. No, I'm terrified. I wonder if we have the real ability to start new, with a fresh breath, without the past choking things out too early. And I worry that he'll start things up again, make me fall in love with him, and then leave me hanging with just the little fragments that are left of my heart.

Because, that's really the issue. I'm terrified that if I keep giving him pieces of my heart, there won't be anything left if things fall apart. Just scattered remains and wishes and tears… and regret. Regret that I tried again when I knew things could go sour. Regret that there wasn't going to be any heart left to give to someone else someday.

Is this going to be just another example of trusting someone, believing in someone, and having the carpet yanked out from under my feet?

I reach down and start rolling up the car window with the hand crank. This car might be adorable, but it would be nice if it had some power.

Just as I'm locking the doors and starting my walk into the hospital, my phone beeps.

Grey: Can't wait to see you, Charlie girl.

I smile. Even if things are a little uneasy right now in my family, at least I'll get to see my sweet little brother in a few weeks.

———

Fifteen hours later, I'm showered, dressed, and waiting for Jeremy to pick me up before we head to Burbank for the game when my phone starts to ring. I dig into my backpack to find it, and when I read the words on my screen, I'm instantly on alert.

Mom Calling

I let out a breath, suck a deep one in for confidence, then lift it to my ear after swiping to accept.

"Hey mom," I say, leaning against the back of the couch. "What's up?"

"Charlotte, dear, how's your day going?" My mother's voice is strained, and I'm instantly on edge wondering what's wrong.

"Things are okay. Just waiting for someone to pick me up so we can go do some volunteer work this morning. How are things with you?" I could kick myself for dropping in the volunteer work comment. Even when I'm living my life my own way, according to my rules, and trying to distance myself from this zombie-Stepford-bride person my mom wants me to be, I still can't help but throw in things to our conversation that I hope will make her proud of me.

"Just getting ready for the annual Scarlet Gala," she says, not addressing my comment. The Scarlet Gala is this large fundraiser my parents put on each year to benefit the local university. It's literally the reddest thing that has ever existed in this world, with every table and centerpiece and decoration the bright color of the university's brand colors, punctuated only by the cream color that is mandatory in the dress code. It's like those fancy White Parties you hear about happening in the south, where people wear all white and drink champagne in the park surrounded by white flowers and sitting on white blankets.

One year, I refused to wear cream, instead putting on a neon green leotard and tutu I'd borrowed from a friend. I was probably in the fourth or fifth grade at the time, but my mother had been so upset. It was like I had ruined everything because I was a kid who liked bright colors. It had sparked a huge fight between her and my dad, who had allowed me to get into the car like that while my mother had been busy at the venue getting final touches completed.

"Well, what would you have had me do, Diana, leave her at home alone?"

My mother had thrown her razor sharp eyes in my direction so hard, it felt like a physical blow. "It would have been better her stay home than let her show up here and cause a ridiculous scene, looking like that." She'd stormed off in a huff, and my sister had laughed. But my brother had reached over and tucked his little hand into mine.

I'm so lost in the memory I don't realize I've missed whatever my mom has been saying.

"Sorry, can you say that again?"

There's a pause. "I said we won't be able to come to your graduation. The Scarlet Gala is just taking up so much time this year, you know, and there really isn't anyone else who can…"

But I stop listening as a sharp ringing starts in my ears.

I can't have heard her correctly. Surely not. There isn't… I can't even believe what I just…

They're not coming to graduation? Is she fucking serious?

I knew things were strained, but I'm their daughter. I'm supposed to be important. *What is happening?*

She's still talking on the other end of the line, but I just let my hand drop from my ear and stare at my cell screen, watching the tiny numbers click by. Before I can think better of it, I hit the giant red X to end the call. Even in my most rebellious times, I've *never* hung up on my mother before.

I don't know how long I'm sitting there, my mind numb, when I hear a knock on the door. I stand woodenly and grab my backpack and water bottle, make sure I have my keys and phone, then slip my shoes on at the door before opening it.

Jeremy stands there with a small smile on his face, but it falls quickly when he sees me.

"What's wrong?"

I just shake my head, push a pair of sunglasses onto my face and give him the best smile I can muster up. "Rough morning. Let's go."

I push him lightly out of the way when he doesn't move, so I can turn and lock the door. But when I start walking out to his SUV, he grabs my wrist and stops me.

"Charlie, what's going on?"

I pull my wrist out of his grip.

"Nothing I want to talk about, okay?" My tense stance deflates slightly at the tenderness and worry on his face. "Like I said, rough morning. I just need to focus on this game and whatever before I think about this, okay?"

When he finally nods, reluctantly I can tell, I turn and walk out to the car where Malory waits for us.

The morning is a blur, which I hate. Combine the exhaustion from my overnight shift with the emotion from hearing my parents are skipping my graduation, and I just feel like one big exposed nerve. I stand on the sidelines with my clipboard and whistle and pen, contributing absolutely nothing but fragile smiles as the team plays their first game. They look so precious in their little blue and black uniforms, and they have so much energy and I want *so* badly to be emotionally present right now. But I just can't.

So I let out a huge sigh of relief when the game is over and the kids and families are all packed up and heading home. I sit quietly in the bleachers and wait as Jeremy finishes up his conversation with Patrick. I keep replaying what my mother said to me, trying, trying so hard to understand where she's coming from. But I just can't.

When Jeremy wraps up and they shake hands, I lug the massive mesh bag of basketballs towards the exit.

"I got it, Char," Jeremy says, taking the bag out of my hands. He's still looking at me with worry, like I'm a wounded animal. And maybe I am. I sure feel like I've been discarded. Maybe hit by a car and left for dead. It's amazing what a few inconsiderate words can do to your psyche.

"Thanks," I say, and then start walking over to his car.

After we've buckled into the backseat and Malory has started driving, Jeremy turns to face me.

"You wanna tell me what's going on, yet?" he asks.

When I sit in silence for too long, he gets impatient.

"I know I might not be able to fix the problem, Charlie, but you're the person who espouses the virtues of talking about your problems. You're the one who always encouraged Rachel to go to therapy, and who called me on my shit for not talking about my own problems. Well, it's time for you to say what's going on."

I take in the encouraging smile on his face and sigh.

"My parents are skipping my graduation."

His head jerks back.

"What?"

I nod. "I know. My mom does this big gala every year to benefit the University, and she said they have too much going on right now to make it." I turn to look at him. "But I know it's just a bunch of bullshit. They don't want to come out here. They don't support me and what I'm doing, so they aren't coming." I shrug and look down at my hands, picking at my nails. "I guess I just always thought that even if they didn't support my choices, they would at least still support *me*. But after what happened with my brother, I shouldn't be surprised, I guess."

Jeremy's silent as I vent, but I can feel the anger simmering from him, radiating towards me.

"I wish there was something I could say to make you feel better, but I know this is just one of those things you have to sort through on your own," he finally says.

I nod but keep my eyes in my lap, which is why I'm startled when Jeremy reaches out and lifts my chin with his hand, bringing my eyes to his.

"But I can tell you this," he says, his face too close to mine and yet not close enough. His face is suddenly so stern, so focused. "Your parents are fucking idiots if they don't realize what they're missing out on. I can promise you that I'll be there, cheering you on as you walk across the stage. You've worked so hard for this, and you deserve to be proud of yourself, pretty girl." He tucks a loose strand of hair behind my ear, his eyes tracking his movements before they come back to looking into my soul, his expression softening. "You are a rainbow that exploded out of a black and white movie. Don't let the fact that someone else is color blind rob you of your ability to brighten the world."

I can't help myself when I lean forward and press my

136

lips against his. He's startled enough to pop backwards for just a second, to look at my face, before he leans forward and crashes his mouth to mine.

It feels like coming home, when I truly don't feel like I've had one in a long time. His tongue caresses mine, sweeping into my mouth and sending euphoria shooting through my veins. He keeps his hands on my face, holding me in place, almost like he's afraid I'm going to back away, chicken out. But I couldn't even if I wanted to.

I moan into his mouth, let my hands reach for him. I grab his shirt and tuck it tightly between my fingers, grabbing onto anything I can find, anything I can grasp that makes this a tangible reality. Where my problems aren't bigger than what's happening right now.

Jeremy breaks the kiss but doesn't let go of my face. He keeps me close, his breath rushing out in pants against my face, the cool mint smell puffing at me as he catches his breath.

"Tell me you actually want me to kiss you right now," he finally says, which is not at all what I expected him to say. "Tell me this isn't just you trying to distract yourself from what's going on with your family."

It takes a second for his words to register, and by the time they do, I must have paused for too long, because Jeremy lets out a sigh and leans backwards in his seat, his hands falling away from me.

"Jeremy…" I start, but can't find the words to say, so I don't say anything. Am I supposed to say that I paused because I was pumped so full of bliss I couldn't translate his words into actual English? I settle back into my own seat, tucking into myself slightly. Or do I say that I don't really know why I kissed him? That it just felt right in the moment and I didn't want to let the moment pass.

"You know as well as I do that using something to numb the pain you're feeling isn't healthy."

I look over to Jeremy, who sits staring out the window.

"You've worked really hard to get to a point where you don't use your body to make things feel better. Isn't that what you told me? That it took you months and months of reminding yourself that your body isn't something you want to trade for a few minutes of feeling good?"

Shame washes over me as I remember the words I spoke to Jeremy just a few weeks ago. How was I so quick to jump back into bad habits? Hadn't I taught myself anything?

"We're here."

Malory's voice breaks the spell I'm under, reminding me that we aren't in the car alone. That someone else is bearing witness to my moment of weakness.

I glance over at Jeremy, but he's already out of the car and rounding my side. I open the door and slide my legs out just as he reaches me, but I avoid his eyes and his attempt to help me out of the car. As he walks me to the door, the silence between us is awkward and uncomfortable.

"Thanks for…"

"If you need…"

We both smile lightly.

"Go ahead," I say.

Jeremy tucks his hands into his hips and leans back on his heels.

"I was just gonna say, if you need anyone to talk to, feel free to give me a call. Okay?"

I nod, feeling uncertain. Because I do want to numb

this ache I feel. But I'm not entirely certain the sadness I feel has anything to do with my family. I want to tell him to come in, but not because his body can make me feel better about the shitty circumstances I've found myself in.

No. I want him to come in because he's the only person I can imagine talking to right now. I want to spend time with him. I want to snuggle next to him while I cry, and get mad at him when he makes jokes to get me to laugh even though I'm in a shitty mood. But just as quickly as these revelations flood into my mind, the reality that it won't happen crashes down.

He's letting me down easy, because he thinks if I reach for him now, it's because of what happened with my family. So, today, I have to let this go. Today, I have to give him a hug, say thank you, and go deal with my problems in a way that works.

And I'll keep focusing on dealing with my problems until I feel like I'm in a better place, just like I told Jeremy to do.

But then?

Once we've both worked through the shit that life has been throwing at us?

Then it'll be time to give in.

CHAPTER FIFTEEN
Jeremy

May

I can't believe she's graduating. My sweet, precious baby sister is going to walk across the stage and shake hands with the president and move her tassel to the other side of her cap.

And then she'll be done. Just like that.

My sister is a pretty amazing person. She's gone through a lot in life and has been strong enough to come out on the other side, full of positivity and drive and determination to succeed. She's gonna enjoy her summer off and then start graduate school in the fall at UCLA. She wants to be a teacher and a high school soccer coach, and I think she's going to absolutely rock at it.

Rachel's boyfriend, Mack, is sitting next to me in the stands, along with Charlie's brother, Greyson. I can promise that I have never felt a punch in the gut like I did when I walked into their apartment this morning and found Charlie wrapped up in another man's embrace.

And I've never felt relief as sweet as finding out it was her brother.

Rachel had a nice little laugh about it and Charlie gave me a little smirk. I can't help it if I wear my feelings on my sleeve, sometimes. Right?

So now, we sit in the stands, us three guys, supporting two important women in our lives as they complete the last step towards an amazing achievement.

I'm thrilled for Rachel, absolutely. But I keep thinking about Charlie, how brave she is for going after what she wants even without her parents' support.

"She's crazy about you, you know."

I turn to my right, where Greyson sits, innocently sipping a coffee that I know is spiked with something. I want to ask for a sip. But instead, I just stare at him.

"Charlie, I mean."

"Yeah," I reply. "I figured that's who you were talking about. I was just surprised you said anything. Aren't you two supposed to have a great bond and hold each others' secrets and all that shit?"

Greyson smiles at me.

"Usually, yes. I know some doozies about that girl that would send me to my grave if she knew I shared them with anyone, let alone you." He chuckles, but then relaxes his face until it's just a soft smile. "She's the only thing that got me through high school, what with how my parents reacted to me coming out."

When my brow furrows, he looks surprised.

"She didn't tell you? My parents basically disowned me when I told them I was gay in the seventh grade. Charlie was the first person to know. I think I told her when I was in the fifth or sixth grade. But the big thing was telling my parents. I knew they were the types to care a lot about what everyone else thought, but I really did think telling them was a good idea. They always seemed to care about everyone, so I just figured that they'd care about me too, even though I wasn't going to be who they originally wanted me to turn into." He shakes his head and takes another sip of his brew. "My father spoke about ten words to me between the time I told them and the day I left for the east coast five years later."

"That must have been hard," I say, unsure what to say other than show him my support. I might have had some shitty circumstances growing up, but even I can't imagine that kind of pain.

He nods. "Yeah. Well, like I said. I had Charlie. Our other sister, Issy, she was too focused on what our parents wanted to realize what was happening to me. When your mind is focusing on towing the line, you don't pay attention when that line is tied like a noose around someone else's neck. But Charlie did everything she could to show me that I was loved. It's probably the only reason I didn't try to find that love somewhere else, you know?"

He sighs. "But it took me a while to realize that Charlie didn't have anyone like that in *her* life. I had her, but who did she have? So she did the thing every self-help book says kids do when they don't get enough love growing up. She tried to find it somewhere else, in somebody else."

My stomach clenches, feeling like there is a space deep in my gut telling me that if I had just realized this about Charlie when we first got together, maybe I could have solved that for her, been the person she needed.

"I'm just glad she finally found it, you know?"

"What do you mean? Found what?"

"Her self-worth," he replies.

I scoff. "Charlie is one of the most confident people I've ever seen."

He just shakes his head. "Confidence and self-worth are completely different things, man. One is a projection for others. The other is an internal need for belonging and love. Confident people have low self-worth all the time, and people who believe intrinsically that they have value and worth aren't always confident. They're apples and oranges."

Just then the announcer welcomes everyone to the 122nd Commencement at Glendale College. The words are clear and crisp over the speakers, but it translates into white noise in my mind. All I can think of is the strong, confident woman getting ready to walk across the stage and accept her diploma. I think about all of the times when she has done everything she can to be supportive and helpful to Rachel, what she has done to support and care about me, even when she probably had barely enough time to for herself.

And I feel this growing impatience. This desire to tell her just how much she means to me. How important she is. How special. My body gets slammed with a restlessness that she needs to know, right now. She needs to hear from me that no matter what happens between us, she will always be someone special. That her decision about me, whatever it is, doesn't take away from how important and loved she is.

"So anyway," Greyson continues, "like I was saying. She's crazy about you. But she's had all these people in her life that haven't really gone to bat for her. People who love her but not enough, not in the way that says she comes first. I mean, look at our fucking parents. They're skipping her graduation because they don't approve of her *nursing degree*. You know how smart you have to be to get through that? All the science classes? Yuck. No thanks. But that's just the life she's lived. She's never been first, she's never been the most important. I think it's why she's always wearing bright colors and drawing attention to herself. She wants the validation it brings when people look at her. But not in a shallow way, you know? It's just that… well, there's always a part of her that will believe she's not enough."

My gut pushes me onto my feet. "I gotta go."

"What?" Mack, who has been on his phone the entire time we've been sitting here, finally adds to the conversation. "Everything is gonna start in a few minutes. Where are you going?"

I let out a breath. "I need to talk to Charlie."

Mack still looks confused, but Greyson has a shit-eating-grin on his face as he holds his coffee cup to his mouth. He nods once, then turns and starts talking to Mack as I push my way through the bleachers in the auditorium.

I fly down the steps and rush through the double doors where greeters are passing out programs. I look left and right and don't see a huge line of people in all black, so I return to the greeters and ask where the graduates are lining up. Then I jog around to the other side. Where I see a massive crowd of students in hats and robes.

"Charlie Davenport?" I'm not screaming or shouting, just speaking loudly as I worm my way through the line trying to find her.

I spend a few minutes scanning the swarm of graduates and weaving through clusters of friends giggling and taking selfies, coming up empty as I hit the front of the line. I take a breath. I had hoped to talk to her before the ceremony, before she walks across the stage, but I can just wait talk to her after.

"Jeremy?"

I look up and there she is, looking both ridiculous and gorgeous in a massive black robe and a stupid hat on her head. I've never felt more right about something than I do in this moment. This isn't about me wanting her to love me. This isn't even about trying to convince her that I'm in love with *her*. This is about making sure she understands, beyond anything, that she isn't alone today.

"I just wanted to talk to you for a second." I push my hand through my hair.

"Okay, yeah. But it looks like we are walking in soon, so..."

I turn and see a woman in a headset looking at the graduates and talking into her microphone, shuffling the first few people around to her liking.

"Okay well... shit, now that I'm here, I feel like a jackass. But I just had to tell you, I just want to make sure you know... you are an amazing person."

Her face softens, dropping from confused to a mixture of sweet and slightly unsure.

"You've lived a life with too many people backing out on you and letting you down. And I just, I wanted... no, I *needed* to tell you this before you walk on that stage. I want to make sure you know, without a doubt, that you have people in this crowd who are proud of you. And who love you, no matter what. You're this kind, caring, thoughtful person who does everything you can to love those around you. You've worked so hard for today. And I just… I hated the thought that you felt alone today. That you felt like no one was here for you. And I just wanted you to know. We're here for you. I'm… I'm here for you. No matter what."

There's dead silence from her as I finish what I have to say. I'm not sure how she's taken it. I know I didn't get the words entirely right, but I just had to get it off my chest. I had to make sure she knew.

"Alright let's go!"

There's a cheer from the students around us, and the line starts moving through the double doors.

I take a step back.

"Have fun out there, okay? You *deserve* it."

Her eyes just watch me as I turn and walk the way I came, weaving in and out of the mass of undergrads so I can get out of this hallway and back to my seat.

"Jeremy!"

I turn when I hear my name, and get nearly knocked to the ground when Charlie slams into me, her arms wrapping around me tightly.

"You need to get back in line," I say with a laugh.

She giggles and I squeeze her tighter, loving the sound.

"I just," she leans back, her hands resting on my arms, mine holding her around the waist, "I just wanted to say thank you. For what you said. And what it means to me."

I smile at her, play with a strand of her hair that's escaped and fallen in front of her cap.

"And I wanted to ask if I can take you on a date."

My eyes fly to hers.

"What?"

She smiles and laughs. "A date. You know… dinner, movie, a trip to the beach. That kind of thing."

I smile back at her, a little shocked and feeling overwhelmingly happy. "Just tell me when," I reply, knowing that playing hard-to-get isn't the right move for this moment. I don't want her doubting things. Ever again.

"Tomorrow night," she replies, her voice dropping as people continue to file past us.

I'm taken back several years at her response. "And what if I have plans tomorrow?" I reply, the grin on my face on the verge of cracking my face in half.

She shrugs and inches closer to me. "Do I sound like a dick if I say you'll make sure you don't have plans tomorrow?"

I huff out a laugh and draw her in for a kiss. Then break away.

"Go! Everyone's almost gone," I say. "I'll see you after."

She just smiles, kisses me again, places a hand on her cap and runs off in the opposite direction, her black cape billowing behind her.

EPILOGUE
Charlie

July

"I want to see it tonight," I say as I spread a blanket out on the sand.

"That's what she said."

I turn and give a seriously intense eye-roll to Jeremy, who is setting down a backpack full of crackers and cheese and other sweet treats.

"Is anything with you not a sex reference?" I ask, brushing off some runaway sand and kicking off my flip flops to sit cross legged on the floral-patterned quilt.

"Nope."

"Okay. That's cool. Just wanted to make sure I know what I'm getting myself into. And if you can't keep up with *my* sex references, I'm not sure this relationship is gonna work out."

He just laughs and plops down next to me, kicking up a bunch of sand in the process.

"Oh, *come on*, I just cleaned it off. It was perfec…"

But my words are cut off by his lips pressing against mine, and I can't help but sigh into what must be our thousandth kiss, but feels brand new every time.

It has been about two months since Jeremy and I finally gave it a shot, since RJ and I graduated from college. And things have been... well, they've been amazing. Absolutely, blow my mind, steal the breath from my lungs, amazing.

After the graduation ceremony, Jeremy and I went out to dinner with Mack, RJ and Greyson. Later that night, once I'd gotten Greyson all settled in my room on a blow up mattress, I went down to the living room, where Jeremy and I had a heart-to-heart. We laid it all out. We hashed through everything that happened my freshman year, talked through our time apart. We talked about RJ. My family. Everything.

And we've been together ever since.

We've also been working on our own personal things, too. Jeremy talked to RJ about the DUI and the alcohol, and the two have started going to AlAnon together, which is for families of people with alcohol problems. I think RJ wants Jeremy to go to an actual AA meeting, but I don't think he's there yet. He hasn't had anything to drink since the DUI, so we'll see how things continue.

Greyson and I flew out to Nebraska to talk to our parents about how they made us feel as kids and now as adults. We did it together, holding hands. It didn't go exactly the way we hoped. Mainly, we assumed they would show us the door. But, in a surprising turn of events, our parents looked ashamed. My mom actually cried, which I haven't seen her do since I was a kid. It's going to take time to adjust to things together, but it's good to know we are moving forward together. As a family.

I pull away from his kiss.

"If you distract me, I might miss it!" I say, slightly breathless.

He just smiles and touches my cheek, kissing me briefly before maneuvering me in his arms to look out at the horizon, tucking me in so my back leans against his chest, his arms around my waist, our fingers linked together.

We sit in silence as the sun drops lower and lower along the horizon. My eyes hurt from glaring at the sun and I keep closing and reopening them again. But I want to see it. The green flash. Every day is a new chance to see it, to see something special. If I don't get to see it today, maybe I'll see it another day.

But with Jeremy's arms around me, I know that the love in my life isn't an illusion. I know I'm loved, not only by him, but by myself as well. And that makes every day feel like a fresh chance at something amazing.

Keep reading for the first chapter of a sweet, single mom, next door neighbor romance:

CHAPTER ONE

Annie

I stare longingly out my kitchen window into my new next-door neighbor's backyard. I can see the smoke coming from his grill, smell the delectable scent of what I can only assume is burgers as it wafts through the air, and I rub my protruding tummy absentmindedly.

I'm pretty sure I've never been this hungry in my entire life, and that includes the week I did some weird juice cleanse because Tricia swore it would help me lose those few extra pounds that I'd put on over Christmas. That was at least five years ago, but I've never forgotten the way my stomach would twist and roll, desperate for something to eat that wasn't a detestable blend of ginger root, celery and agave. Or something else equally as heinous.

But right this minute, I would bet every single dollar I have, swear on my life, on my *mother's* life, that those burgers were sent to this earth as a divine gift from above. Unfortunately, a divine gift for my neighbor, and not for me, which is where my quandary lies.

I've only been in this house for a week. One incredibly long and emotionally exhausting week where we've eaten nothing but takeout and fast food, with the local 7-Eleven workers already greeting me by name on my morning run for a decaf coffee. One week of a new life in a new house, in a not-so-new state where I've been trying to unpack and get things settled for me and Jones, while also fighting the desire to burst into tears and collapse on the bed (or couch, or floor) at any given moment.

So, needless to say, I haven't really been able to go grocery shopping to fill my cupboards with the healthy stuff a good mother should feed her kid.

And now it's getting late on a Sunday afternoon at the end of what I am sure is only the first of many more incredibly long and emotionally exhausting weeks in this new life of ours.

And I'm hungry.

Starving, actually.

Close to bursting into tears at how badly I want that burger.

Objectively, there's probably nothing special about it. Apart from being a direct gift from Jesus himself, it really is just meat over a fire.

But just go ahead and try to tell that to my pregnant brain. Tell that to this human lounging around inside of me, yanking on the umbilical cord and throwing out demands like she's J.Lo.

"I hear you!" I shout at my stomach. "But we don't always get what we want!"

And then I catch another whiff, but this time of something else. Is that...? It smells like baked potatoes. I *love* baked potatoes.

I glance back out my kitchen window, which overlooks my backyard and gives me a decent view of my neighbor's, and feel like if I don't get to eat whatever is being made next door, I'll collapse.

Just right here, in my kitchen, I'll drop to the floor and waste away into nothing.

Which I know is a stupid thought because even though I've barely had a banana all day, with the way this little monster inside of me is sprawled out, resting comfortably on all of my organs and pressing into my bladder and stomach, it feels like I just finished stuffing my face.

I'm sure when my mom drops Jones off in the next thirty minutes, he'll be hungry too. And if I don't have a plan for dinner, she'll hover and try to make us food even though there's still nothing in the pantry for anyone to cook.

And then I'll get the sympathetic look. The one that says, *Oh honey, do I need to go grocery shopping for you? Are you really capable of handling this by yourself?* And then she'll be inviting herself to handle things and move in and take over and I just...

Nope. No thank you. Not going to happen.

I love my mama. She is my rock. She has been there for me through so many ups and downs, and I can't imagine my life without her.

But I moved out at eighteen for a reason, and that was because Marybeth McAllister is the nosiest busybody to ever busy herself into anybody's business. And an eighteen-year-old woman who wanted to enjoy some freedom would not have survived under Marybeth's watchful eye.

So, no. I can't let my mom come back from her

grandma-and-me day with Jones to a barren dinner table, because I can't deal with any questions or concerns anymore. I just can't deal with it today.

When I consider my options, I know that not only do I not have enough mental strength to go grocery shopping, but I also don't have the time to go pick anything up before they get home.

And realistically, the only thing my brain can focus on is the smell of those fucking burgers.

I feel like a zombie as I grab a Tupperware bowl out of an open box on the kitchen floor and make my way through my house. I know I should have spent the day getting things organized, putting things away, and trying to make sure that Jones and I are settling comfortably into our new house.

Well… a rented shack is a bit more accurate, but beggars can't be choosers. And I really did have the best of intentions when I started unpacking this morning.

But the third box I opened, completely by accident, was filled with Andrew's shirts.

They still smell like him.

And regardless of everything that's happened, everything that I've found out and been through over the past few months – the past eight years, if I'm completely honest – he was all that I'd known. And now he's gone.

So instead of getting through the list of things I absolutely needed to get done, like going grocery shopping or setting up the cable or scheduling an appointment with a new OB/GYN, or even finding a local mechanic to take a look at my barely functioning '98 Toyota Camry, I chose to crawl into bed and snuggle with a pillow and let out the week's worth of tears that had been building up with no outlet for release.

Because when you suddenly become a single parent to a 4-year-old and have another on the way that's just about done cooking… and when you don't have a real job or any friends or any way to actually keep your life afloat… you just don't have the time to stop and cry in the shower. Hell, you're lucky enough if you *get* a shower.

But that means today is nearly a full day wasted, and I have to figure out what to do for dinner for my kid.

So with only one thing on my mind, I clutch the Tupperware bowl tightly to my chest, walk out of my front door and down the three steps and tiny path, along the sidewalk, and then up the pathway and few steps to my neighbor's door.

I noticed this house when I moved in last week. I've always wanted a gray house with a black door, and that's what my neighbor has. It isn't the most amazing house I've ever seen, but it looks like someone takes care of it, since the exterior looks freshly painted and a bunch of beautiful plants line the windows.

My rental looks like something out of The Great Depression in comparison. The grass is brown, since California is just about always in a drought. The paint on the tan exterior is chipped and flaking away, leaving a scattering of dandruff around the house's perimeter. There are bars on the windows and a security gate on the door, which makes me feel just as safe as can be. And there are no plants because, like I said, *drought*.

But it's mine and Jones', and it's what I can afford with how everything panned out after…

Well… just, after.

I take a deep breath and knock on the beautiful black

door.

The second I'm done, I regret my decision. I feel like an idiot. I don't know these people. I'm just the crazy new neighbor standing at their door with a bowl, hoping for some food? What the hell was I thinking? They are going to think I'm absolutely certifiable, and then someone's gonna wonder if I'm even capable of taking care of my child. I can't believe...

But before I can talk myself into slipping back over to my house with no one the wiser, I hear, "Hold on a second!" shouted from somewhere behind the door.

Should I still run away? I bet if I waddled fast enough, I could make it back to my...

My thoughts die as the door opens. The man that emerges is very nice looking and probably about ten years older than me. Back in high school, I probably would have swooned and might have cared that he was seeing me with red-rimmed eyes, a gross hairball knotted high on my head, sans-shower and barefoot holding a glass bowl at his door.

But these aren't my high school years. And while I might normally have too much pride to ask for anything, I feel too beaten down today to care what he thinks of me. I mean, really, I feel like he should just feel thankful that I've shown up at his door wearing pants.

He gives me a pleasant but neutral smile. "Can I help you?" he asks, his eyebrows tightening just enough for me to see that he wonders if he should be welcoming or concerned.

Definitely concerned, I think to myself.

I clear my throat.

Then clear it again.

"I'm sorry to just show up like this," I finally manage to croak out, "but what you're cooking smells so good, and this pregnancy makes me a complete whacko when I smell something that smells as amazing as whatever it is that's coming out of your backyard. I haven't been able to go grocery shopping yet since we just moved in – I'm Annie, by the way – and we don't have a grill anymore because that was…".

And to my absolute horror, tears begin to fill my eyes, and I know that the word vomit is just going to spill forth.

"… that was my ex's thing, grilling the food. I never really figured out what I was doing and I'd just burn everything to a crisp, you know? But he was so good at it, and anyway I don't have a grill and I haven't been able to go pick anything up and I was just wondering if you wouldn't mind sharing? Maybe? Because if my mother comes back with Jones and sees we have no food, she'll just make herself at home and I don't even know if I can handle that on top of everything else."

I take a deep breath to continue, but stop when the guy puts up a hand to stop me.

"Sorry," I say again, almost on a whisper, still gripping my Tupperware bowl so tightly my fingers are surely white, wiping the tears away with my free hand.

God, what must he think of me? He probably has guests or a family and I'm standing here asking him for food and crying about my dead ex-boyfriend not being able to grill me a burger?

I'm definitely a lunatic.

"You said your name is Annie?" he finally asks, after an elongated pause in which I'm sure he's considering calling the cops.

I glance up at him and manage a watery smile. Nodding, I say, "Annie McAllister. My son Jones and I live next door." I point at the depression house a few yards away.

He glances at our house next door, then back at me, and extends his hand, which I just now realize he has been wiping on a dirty rag since he answered the door.

"I'm Cole," he says. "Cole Lannigan."

I shift my grip on the Tupperware to one hand and stick out my other to take his. It's warm and large, engulfing mine. It should be intimidating, but all I feel is an overwhelming sense of calm.

"Hi Cole," I say.

He gives me a smile that hovers between sympathetic and concerned – two of my least favorite things – but I can at least see it's genuine.

"Hi Annie. It's great to meet you. So, here's what I'm thinking," he says, taking his hand back and leaning against the doorframe, crossing his arms over his chest. The move draws my eyes to his biceps, which I belatedly realize are covered in tattoos. But I don't spend time lingering on his ink, my eyes returning to his. How can I when I have the overwhelming force of his gaze laser focused on me? "How about you head on home, and I'll pack all of this food up and bring it over once it's done?"

My jaw drops.

"I'm making way too much to feed just myself, and I'm happy to help if my cooking – as subpar as it may be – might be able to solve the problem. I know I need all the help I can get when my parents swing through town, so I can definitely jump in if it gets you out of a jam."

He says all this while he stands there, looking calm as can be, still in repose against the doorjamb.

I fight the urge to look behind me to make sure I'm the only person standing on his tiny porch. Because he can't seriously be talking to me about coming over for dinner and bringing all of his food... can he?

When I just stare at him, he smiles again. But this time, his caramel colored eyes show a hint of warmth and brightness that wasn't there before.

"Did I lose you, Annie?"

"No," I manage to spit out. "No, you didn't lose me, I..." I take a deep breath and let it out slowly. "I just wasn't expecting... anything. I don't know, I was just... thank you."

I laugh. Just a tiny chuckle, barely a snicker. There isn't really any humor in it, but it's the first laugh I've let free in who knows how long that wasn't directed at my son.

I lock eyes with him. "Thank you so much, Cole. You have no idea... absolutely no idea how much I needed something like this today. Thank you."

He just continues to smile at me, so patient as I thank him profusely, and in a way that doesn't do real justice to how I feel.

"No problem, Annie. You head on home. I'm just finishing up, so I'll be over with the food in about fifteen minutes. Sound good?"

I just nod at him, and then turn and speed-walk back down his steps as fast as my massively pregnant body can carry me before he can think any better of his decision to spend the evening with his crazy neighbor and her son.

I glance over as I get to my door and see that he's

still standing at his own, watching me. I give him a small wave, which he returns with one of those masculine head nods, and then fling my door open and rush inside.

Ten minutes later, I hear my mom's car pull up on the street out front. I've just finished the most impressive feat I think I've ever pulled off in such a small amount of time.

I managed to set the table.

Sure, there are still boxes everywhere, even if I've tried to shove them into corners and tuck their top flaps in so as not to seem so haphazard. Nothing has been put away, there is still no food in the fridge, and there's nothing to actually eat on the table yet, but I was able to pull out and rinse off some real plates and utensils and cups and place them around the kitchen table that sits in the breakfast nook.

For a lady who tried to feed her son chicken nuggets with wooden chopsticks yesterday, I think it's looking pretty spectacular.

I'm pushing the last box into a non-hiding spot that I think will somehow disguise the insanity that is my kitchen when I hear the front door open.

"I'm here!"

I smile when I hear Jones' voice. He looks so much like Andrew that sometimes it makes me want to burst into tears just looking at him. But I don't want him to have a mom who does nothing but cry whenever she sees him. I can't imagine what it would do to me if someone cried every time they looked at me. Talk about developing a complex, am I right?

So when my little guy comes barreling through the house and into the kitchen, I squat as low as I can manage at 30 weeks and open my arms wide so I can catch him when he comes flying at me. And when he hits me, I go top over tail and splay flat on my back, with Jones tucked safely in my arms.

"Careful of mama's tummy, remember?" I say, shifting him to the side slightly but still holding him close.

His little face looks so stricken for a moment, and he puts his little hand on my stomach and gives it a light kiss, whispering "sorry guppy" before turning back to look at me.

"You have fun with Mimi?" I ask, and his eyes instantly brighten.

"We went to the zoo!" he shouts in my face. "I got to pet a turtle and a monkey threw his poo at us."

"Oh, wow! Sounds amazing. But," I pull him closer and give him a sniff. "I don't smell anything."

"*No*, mom, there was a *window* so the poop didn't hit us," Jones says, cracking up in that little kid way that just destroys your soul and makes you wish you had ten kids. When he laughs like that, I forget that our lives are anything other than perfect.

"You sure?" I sniff him again. "Actually I think I smell something." He squirms and giggles in my arms "Yep. You smell like monkey poo, little dude." He continues to laugh and wriggle his little body around as I tickle his stomach.

A throat clearing is the only indication that we're not alone. When I turn my head, I see my mom standing at the kitchen entrance holding a plate of burgers. And standing behind her, practically filling the doorway, is

Cole.

"I found this gentleman at your door when Jones and I got back," she says, and then one eyebrow rises so high I fear it might get lost in her forest of honey blonde hair. "He said he was coming over for dinner?"

She says it like it's one question that only has one answer. But what no one else would know is that there isn't one answer because there isn't just one question. There are at least ten questions in what she just said, but unfortunately for the busybody she is, she won't be getting the answers to any of them this evening.

"As I said outside, Mrs. McAllister, Annie and I got to talking and I offered to cook us dinner as a welcome-to-the-neighborhood," he says, giving me a wink. "Where should we put the good stuff?"

I get up as ungracefully as I'm sure can be imagined from my place sprawled on the shitty linoleum in my kitchen and motion to the table.

"Here's great," I say with a small smile, still unbelieving that Cole is here and he brought food.

How does begging for food turn into a sit-down dinner for us and our new neighbor?

Cole seems immune to the laser eyes my mom is observing him with as he sets a ridiculous amount of stuff on the table. A stack of paper plates, red solo cups, a box of plastic forks and knives, a bunch of baked potatoes – *I knew it!* – buns, cheese, various burger toppings and sides. I don't know how he managed to carry it all. I would have had to make at least three trips.

Then my mom walks over and sets the most delicious looking, amazing smelling plate full of burger patties down on the table with a plop.

My mouth is watering so hard, I'm surprised I'm not drooling.

Cole turns then and looks down at my Jones, giving him that same warm smile that disarmed me in seconds. My son has his arms wrapped around my thigh and he's positioned slightly behind me, as if he's using my thigh as a temporary shield. I place a hand on his head and go to introduce Jones to Cole, but the man beats me to it.

"Hey mister," he says, crouching down to Jones' level. "I brought over some burgers for you and me to eat. But before we dig in, I wanted to check with you and see if it's cool if your mom has some too?"

He says it as if he and Jones are already friends, like they've been talking about burgers on a regular basis. It's one of the strangest things I've ever seen, especially because it works.

Jones isn't a big fan of strangers, and I could tell he was startled when Cole just seemed to waltz into our house unannounced. But those big eyes of his seemed to ignite with excitement when Cole leaned down to get his permission to let me join in for dinner.

I was crying earlier today, feeling like a completely lost and miserable mess, and now I'm ready to break into laughter.

This day has seen quite the range of emotions.

I see Jones look up at me, mull it over, then glance at my tummy briefly before looking back to Cole.

"She has the guppy in her tummy. I think she needs food," he finally replies.

Cole gives him a stern look.

"Makes total sense, man. I like your thinking."

Then Cole sticks his hand out and Jones gives him a

low five.

I glance at my mom, who is watching the two interact with bemusement on her face. Then, the nosiest busybody I know does something completely unexpected.

"Well, it looks like everything is under control. I'll just head off to dinner with the girls." She leans forward and gives me a peck on the cheek. "Bye Jonesie," she adds, giving him a smooch on his cheek that he immediately wipes away. "Cole, I'm assuming I'll be seeing you around," she adds, wiggling her fingers at him in a wave before strutting off to the front of the house.

When I hear the front door open and then close, I let out a sigh. I should have given her a better goodbye – you know, given her a hug, a really big one, and a kiss, made plans to do something soon – but I can't seem to be anything other than thankful that she's not hovering like a bee. It's what she does most nights, *just making sure everything is okay Annie Bananie,* even as I'm trying to shoo her out the door. I'm glad to be back near my mom, but we've only been here a week and I'm already desperate for some space.

I look back at Cole, who is taking charge, walking Jones around the table so he can take what he wants before getting him settled into his chair. Jones looks so comfortable with him, so happy and calm, even though he's never seen the man before in his life.

There's a part of me that enjoys seeing Jones like this. But there's another part of me that's dying inside. How can I enjoy seeing another man with my son? Andrew has been gone for barely three months. Even though every day is torture and feels like it lasts too long, three months is nothing in the grand scheme of things. Am I being disloyal to his memory by allowing someone else into my home? To bond with our son?

My thought process doesn't feel like there's a lot of logic to it, mostly because Cole is obviously not trying to be Jones' dad, just a friendly adult. But I can't help the bunny trail my brain is doing right now. I have a smile on my face but there are literal tears streaming down my cheeks. It's safe to say that logical, rational thought processes aren't really my forte right now.

Cole glances over and sees me standing awkwardly in the middle of the kitchen, being a total mess, and he gives me that sympathetic smile again.

Get your shit together, Annie. You have a human child that relies on you for things. And a very nice neighbor here that's feeding you and your son. Stop being a crazy lady.

I wipe my face off on my shirtsleeve, because I'm classy like that, and step forward with a smile, grabbing a paper plate from the stack Cole brought over.

"Thanks for bringing plates," I say, even though the ceramic plates I rinsed off are still out on the table.

"Easier cleanup," he replies with a little shoulder shrug as he takes a seat to the right of Jones at the table. He moves the ceramic plates into a pile and sets them off to the side, then places Jones' paper plate in front of him.

I just nod and put together my burger, then sit down on the seat that has a special pad for my pregnant butt to sit on. I let out an internal sigh, thankful that I kept this after my pregnancy with Jones. I don't know about all the other pregnant ladies in the world, but *damn* do I have a sore ass. All. The. Time. Like, seriously all the time. How are pregnant women around the world sitting anywhere all day, everyday? It would be torture.

I take a decent size bite of my burger, proud of myself for not shoving the whole thing in my mouth at once, and watch Jones and Cole interact. Jones is telling Cole about his trip to the zoo, and Cole is looking at Jones like he is telling the most interesting story he's ever heard. Which is both wonderful and heartbreaking at the same time, because even as I search through my deepest memories, I can't once remember Andrew giving Jones this type of undivided attention.

When Jones gets to the part about the monkey poo, I know I should say something to him about mentioning literal feces at the dinner table, but it feels so good to see him ramble on and on and have someone other than me give him the attention he deserves, that I let it slide.

"Let's ask your mom," is the phrase that yanks me out of my zoned out state.

My eyes lift from Jones to Cole, my brow furrowing. "Wha..?" I begin.

And I shit you not, the entire half-chewed bite of burger falls out of my mouth and onto my plate.

I. Am. Fucking. *Mortified.*

I immediately slap my hand over my mouth, as if that will erase the past five seconds.

This Cole guy has got to be questioning his life right now. Or at least questioning whether I'm fit to be a parent, or wondering how I've survived this long in life.

My cheeks are so warm that they must be glowing, and it doesn't help that both Jones and Cole are giggling and smiling at me.

Suddenly it's all too much, and I burst into tears.

But I'm laughing, too.

I feel like a crazy person.

Absolutely nuts.

Today has been a really rough day.

I can't remember the last time I laughed and cried so much in a twenty-minute period of time.

I rest my elbows on the table and plant my wet, sobby face in my palms and continue to cry and laugh and let it all out on the table.

I feel like I've given the term *airing your dirty laundry for the neighbors* a bountiful new meaning.

When I finally manage to part my fingers and peek at the two boys at the table, I see that Jones is happily dipping French fries into mayonnaise – he learned *that* disgusting habit from his father – and Cole is watching me, a small smile still on his face.

The fact he hasn't left a Cole-shaped hole in the wall as he high tails it back to his own house is a flat-out miracle.

I close my fingers back up and hide behind my hands for a second longer. Then I stand from the table, go to the kitchen sink, rinse off my face, pat it dry with a paper towel, and return to my seat.

"So," I say, lifting up my burger. "What were you talking about?"

And I take a new bite. That I chew fully. And swallow. In its entirety.

Cole grins at me, then looks to Jones.

"You wanna ask?"

Jones nods his little bobble head a million times then looks to me.

"Can I go swimming at Cole's after dinner?" he asks.

My heart breaks a tiny bit.

We had a pool at our old house outside of Chicago.

I've always considered it completely impractical to have a pool when you live somewhere that freezes the wax inside your ear so quickly it feels like you have an ear infection. But when Andrew and I were looking for houses, he mentioned that he'd always wanted a pool growing up, but his parents didn't want to deal with the upkeep. It was one of those random facts you learn about someone that you think you'll forget, but for some reason I've always remembered.

When our realtor took us to the beautiful yellow house on Maple Street in Winnetka – the house we moved into when I was pregnant, the house we lived in when Jones was born, the house we lived in when everything fell apart and I was left trying to pick up all of the pieces – I knew immediately that the pool was going to seal the deal.

Jones has asked a few times about getting a pool since we moved here last week. California seems like a more realistic place to have a pool, with the desert and beach weather, but he doesn't understand that I can't just add a pool to a rental. He doesn't understand what a *rental* is. He just knows this is our new home, and that he misses swimming and his old house and his dad.

So, when Jones asks if he can go swimming, I feel the guilt. The guilt that comes with being a single parent, the guilt that comes when you try to alleviate the pain of losing someone by giving in to what your kid wants.

And even though we don't know Cole at all, and it's a little too chilly outside to go swimming, I smile at my sweet boy and say yes.

Continue reading this sweet, single mom, next door neighbor romance in Like You Mean It, available now on Amazon and free in Kindle Unlimited!

ACKNOWLEDGMENTS

Acknowledgements are so fun to write, because there are always so many amazing people to thank for helping me finish a book.

First, I could NOT have done this without my husband. He continues to be my rock in life, even through both of us having some pretty sucky health problems over the past six months. Babe, I appreciate you so much - your support, your willingness to read the stupid shit I write, and your relentless optimism that I can do anything I set my mind to.

I can't do a section like this and not thank my mom and sister. They are wonderful beta readers and editors for me, and are always willing to give that honest feedback I so need.

I also think it is so important to thank my amazing J Crew team! You are all amazing, and I thank you for your support.

And of course, my amazing readers. Your reviews, your messages, your requests for the next one - they make me smile more than you'll ever know.

Writing a book is scary, because so much of yourself gets put into it. But the encouragement and support I receive makes me feel like revealing myself in an intimate way like this is worth it.

Love your faces!!

MORE FROM JILLIAN

For an up-to-date list of titles, visit:
www.jillianliota.com/books

For bonus content, visit:
www.jillianliota.com/bonus

ABOUT THE AUTHOR

Jillian Liota published her first romance novel in 2016. Since then, she has become known for writing stories filled with emotion, real-world themes, and most importantly, love. She has had her writing praised for depth of character, strong female friendships, deliciously steamy scenes, and positive portrayal of mental health.

Jillian is a Southern California native currently residing in Suwanee, Georgia, where she lives with her husband and three-legged pup.

To connect with Jillian:

Join her **Reader Group** Check out her **Website**
Sign up for her **Newsletter** Send her an **Email**
Rate her on **Goodreads** Stalk her on **Instagram**
Visit her on **Facebook** Add her on **Amazon**

www.ingramcontent.com/pod-product-compliance
Lightning Source LLC
Chambersburg PA
CBHW021042130626
46552CB00005B/1977